Strawberries And Cigarettes

AF080761

KAJAL KUKREJA

BlueRose ONE.com
Stories Matter
NewDelhi • London

BLUEROSE PUBLISHERS
India | U.K.

Copyright © Kajal Kukreja 2024

All rights reserved by author. No part of this publication may be reproduced, stored in a retrieval system or transmitted in any form or by any means, electronic, mechanical, photocopying, recording or otherwise, without the prior permission of the author. Although every precaution has been taken to verify the accuracy of the information contained herein, the publisher assumes no responsibility for any errors or omissions. No liability is assumed for damages that may result from the use of information contained within.

BlueRose Publishers takes no responsibility for any damages, losses, or liabilities that may arise from the use or misuse of the information, products, or services provided in this publication.

BlueRose ONE.com
Stories Matter
NewDelhi • London

For permissions requests or inquiries regarding this publication, please contact:

BLUEROSE PUBLISHERS
www.BlueRoseONE.com
info@bluerosepublishers.com
+91 8882 898 898
+4407342408967

ISBN: 978-93-6452-956-3

Cover Design: Sadhna Kumari
Typesetting: Pooja Sharma

First Edition: August 2024

To everyone who wanted the villain to get the girl.

For everyone who wanted the villain to get the girl.

PLAYLIST

Strawberries and Cigarettes

Troye Sivan

24/7, 365

Elijah Woods

Hate How Much I Love You

Conor Maynard

So High School

Taylor Swift

Boyfriend

Ariana Grande

People You Know

Selena Gomez

i hate you, i love you

Gnash, Olivia O'Brian

idfc

Blackbear

Obsessed

Mariah Carrey

Shameless

Camila Cabello

Gorgeous

Taylor Swift

Señorita

Shawn Mendes, Camila Cabello

SYNOPSIS

"In all the world there's no heart for me like yours. In all the world, there's no love for you like mine."

Siddhant 'Flawless' Goenka, is a cold, ruthless billionaire. A villain with all the looks of a Greek God. With an IQ of 150, he is a genius.

"I googled 'who gives a fuck' and my name wasn't in the search results."

Until he sees her, where all he gives, is a damn fuck.

Kiara 'Queen' Ahuja, is a smart, strong-headed, bold millionaire. An angel by looks and a boss at work, she is always the hardest worker in the room.

"Me? Jealous of you? Bless your delusional heart!"

Until she meets him, where all she is, jealous of his delusional heart.

He is the reason for her ***anger.***

He is the reason for her ***sleepless nights.***

He is her biggest ***competition.***

She is the reason for his ***smile.***

She is the reason for his ***calm slumber.***

She is his ***life.***

Kiara can't bear the face of Siddhant, while hers is the only face he wants to see in every business event. He loves her attention, while she's bothered by his existence.

Is it just a physical attraction as she says, or more?

CONTENTS

Chapter 1

KIARA

I WISH THERE WAS A PROFESSION CALLED READING. And I'd be a billionaire if it was a paid parity. Though I'd still earned enough to buy as many books as I wanted.

I got up from my bed to go back to my original profession. The Ahuja Group was one of the biggest architectural groups in the country, and I kept working to make sure it remained one. Finishing my daily chores, I went outside and found breakfast set on the table. I smiled at Lata Didi, "Didi, how is your daughter? Is she liking the school?"

"Of course, she is. I am so glad she got a chance to study at a missionary school." I nodded and finished my breakfast quickly. "I'll be late tonight, don't make my dinner."

"Okay," I heard her answer as I picked up my bag. I wasn't a fashion freak, but a black coat suited me more than any other outfit. I dialed my stylist to get an outfit ready for tonight, it was the *Business Awards*.

I reached my cabin and got my to-do list for the day ready.

Meeting with Khanna's.

Update staff meeting on the project.

Attend the awards.

The day wasn't hectic. I waited in the conference room for the Khanna's to arrive. They were trying to buy some time from me since I had been constantly achieving good projects.

"Good noon, Ms. Ahuja," Naitik Khanna, the younger son and the most arrogant one from the family wished. I nodded and shook hands with him.

"Afternoon, Mr. Khanna,"

They settled on the seats in front of me and Naitik started explaining the changes he required in his office. The renovation required a good amount of brain and I loved it. Everything that had something to challenge, I was up for it.

"Mr. Khanna, the cabin that your son shared, requires a lot of architectural setup and might take slightly more time than the whole we planned," I informed Mr Khanna as Naitik told him his idea. He sighed, "I do not have a lot of time Ms Ahuja. Naitik, you need to take down some ideas."

"Dad, Goenka's can do it in time." I looked up, as soon as he finished with the name. Did he just compare me with the Goenka's?

Goenka's. The billionaire. The self-made super-architectural brain. A PAIN IN ASS, SID-

I didn't let my thoughts continue and stood up from my seat. "Mr. Naitik Khanna, if you think you can crack a deal with them, please go ahead. I need to have clients who respect my time and know my value."

"I am sorry, Ms. Ahuja." Mr. Khanna stood up too. "Apologies on Naitik's behalf. Take how much time you require, we're signing this with you."

Naitik glared at me as I rolled my eyes and settled down. I looked at my assistant who got the contract made. I signed it first and passed it to the father-son duo who followed. I smirked at Naitik taking it.

"Thank you, Ms. Ahuja," Mr. Khanna nodded and shook hands with me, leaving the room. He was pissed off with his son. I smiled and opened the file again. "Do not mess with me like that again," I looked at Naitik who grudged and went towards the gate.

"Do not mess with Kiara Ahuja again, or I know the exact components on how buildings dissolve into sand." I felt myself scoff and he left the room instantly.

I gulped down a glass of water and went to the presentation room, as the staff reached there to update me with the project. Sitting on the chair, I waited for them to start.

Two hours and a hundred debates later, we finally decided to call the meeting off. Everyone in my team was a hardworking individual and I appreciated my HR for picking the best people. I took the last round of interviews myself, but they made sure I didn't work a lot for it.

I reached my cabin to find my stylist ready with an outfit. A sapphire blue floral gown set into a monochrome floral surface enhanced with metallic glass beads and with cutwork detailing on the sleeves. I loved it.

I smiled at my stylist and slipped into it. The hair and makeup were done accordingly and I looked decently beautiful to be a contender for the Businesswoman of the Year. I had practiced my not-winning-but-happy-for-the-winner-face, and I knew I'd nail it.

I settled in my car, I'd love to drive but the gown could've been a challenge. And I preferred no risks today, I was already nervous. Nervous would be a smaller word, I was on pins and needles until the results were announced.

The event started with some performances and different awards. The most important award was kept for the last and so was my agitation.

"Business of the Year goes to the Goenka Group." I heard and clapped softly. Ahuja Group was a nominee but there was no way my company was higher than his.

Black hair. Blue eyes. Cold demeanor.

There he stood, collecting the award on behalf of his company. He was the only one who could collect it. Goenka Group was one of the fastest-growing architectural groups in India, due to his genius brain and creative head.

Siddhant *'Asshole'* Goenka, I looked at him walking down the stage as he looked at me and our eyes met. Those blue eyes felt like a deep sea, where I'd drown. A known scent of masculine spice and vinegar filled me as he sat on the table next to mine. I didn't look in his direction, ignorance is the best he can get from me.

"Businessman of the Year, well, Businesswoman of this Year goes to, my dearest, the most beautiful woman I know, Kiara Ahuja." I heard Gauri say. She was one of the oldest business partners and earliest shareholders in my company. I had bought back almost all the shares of my company when it hit the million, but she still held a little from it. I smiled and went to the stage, accepting the award from her.

Winning this award once was a chance, winning it thrice is an achievement. "Thank you very much for having me here. Congratulations to every entrepreneur present here. This one's for my team, the Ahuja Group. Enjoy the evening." I spoke over the mic and hugged Gauri. We spoke and laughed as we reached the end of the stage and Gauri's husband passed his hand to her. I walked down myself, my posture straight and confident.

I reached my table and my eyes met the blue orbs, I looked back at the trophy and sat down. I didn't look back until the evening ended.

Chapter 2

SIDDHANT

Businesswoman of the Year, I was a nominee, but I knew I wouldn't win. The deserving, the best, the most likely won, three years in a row. Ms. Kiara Ahuja, somebody who hated me, and had given me enough reasons to do the same.

Chocolate hair. Green eyes. Velvet scent.

The amount of hatred she felt for me was way lesser than what I felt. Three years in a row, three years of her establishing the Ahuja Group, three years of me working my ass off for the Goenka Group, three years of her deciding something, I wish I could have changed.

Her eyes met mine twice in the whole event, but she never let me consume a second more of it. This woman was elayne. Elayne to my life, *once*.

The event ended and everyone got up to leave. Kiara was walking right in front of me, yet I made no sound to distract her. Her velvet scent entered my body and it felt like a signature. Everything about her could drive any man on the Earth crazy, and I wasn't an alien. History doesn't repeat, and so I wouldn't repeat my actions.

I will try not to.

Shrugging my thoughts away, I drove back home. It was sure that Goenka Group was winning the best business this year, our profits were touching the sky. This company had been on top of the charts since the time we started. The shareholders in the start were enormous and thus I could get into various important connections in the country. How did I find the shareholders? They were the people my father robbed.

Shaking my head at fate, I entered the house. Loud music played on the systems and a man danced in the middle of the hall, with 3 girls surrounding him.

ARYAN!

I am tired of this man. Only if he wasn't the closest thing I had to a family, I would've killed him.

I sighed and went near the center table he danced on. "Aryan!"

"Honey, you're home!" I rolled my eyes. I wish he wasn't a writer. "Congratulations on the business award!" He chirped and jumped off the table. Hugging me, "So proud of you!"

"Huh!" My face was colder than ice and I sat down, loosening my tie. "I didn't ask if you want dinner, do you want to eat anything?" His body settled beside mine. I shook my head, "No."

“What are these girls here for?” I asked as the music stopped and the girls settled on the couch. “Do you prefer any?”

“No,” I answered quicker than required. He passed me a smile and looked at the girls. “Girls, let’s call it a night,” he announced. “Mr. Siddhant Goenka is not in the mood today.” He teased me.

“In what mood did you expect me to be? A threesome?” He chuckled. “If you wish so, master.” He croaked and I rolled my eyes. The girls disappeared into the air while he got up.

“Alright, I’ve to write, I’ll be in the study.” I nodded and he left.

Aryan and I had been living together after I established Goenka Group in Mumbai. He was a writer and helped me when I started Goenka Group. His books have been the bestsellers for two years and I am so proud of this charming boy.

He is irritating, but the **best** friend you could ever ask for.

I freshened up into sweatpants and tee and went to the study where he did his work . “How is the planning going on?” He asked.

“It’s going well, but I assume Oberois are approaching the Ahuja Group as well.” I grumbled. He smirked and nudged his knee into mine. “What!?”

“You’re glad, aren’t you?”

“I am not!” I defended. “It’s a bad thing to include her in this.”

"It's a perfect idea, move ahead with the business, Sid!" He suggested and I knew he wasn't talking about *business*. I sighed and shook my head, "This is not how I work, Aryan."

"Fuck your work methods,"

"Mind your language," I hissed. He snickered before typing some words into his laptop. "Sweetie, don't talk about language to me. And also, it has been three years. Do you not understand that there's a thing called moving on?"

"I know, but some people do not."

"Then teach them how to," He countered and I looked at the file kept on my table. "You're going to ruin it."

"I'm the one solving it." He proudly grudged and I controlled a smile. "Move ahead with the *business*."

Business.

Let's get back to business. It's time to get what's mine.

Chapter 3

KIARA

I entered the house and sighed. Siddhant was walking right behind me, he didn't make any sound, but his spicy vinegar smell wasn't unknown. I always knew it was him.

Hi, Siddhant, and you are?

I entered the shower and the memories flowed down as water flowed down on my head. I do not want to go back to the same chain of memories again, in which I have to find a way to blame him.

It was a perfect day, I had won the third Businesswoman and I was going to celebrate it by reading the whole day tomorrow. It was the best plan.

Reading.

The hobby I adored the most. Romance books and romantic fictional men, the best thing I'd ever come across. Tomorrow's plan was set.

What was better than tomorrow? Tonight's reading plan! It has been a while since I'd been up all night to see the enemies fall in love. Uh huh, tonight was the day.

I wiped myself and wore a tee and shorts, picking up *Better Than The Movies*, I walked downstairs to get some coffee.

The air was pulled out of my lungs as soon as I saw who was already present in my hall.

Mom. Dad. Shanaya.

I am so OVER.

They looked at me and shouted delightfully. *Delightfully? Come on!*

My legal parents were waiting for me with a bottle of champagne. Why? They didn't come last year. Is it because it's the third and they finally believe I could achieve it? Oh sure it is!

"Kiara! There you are!" Mom grinned and I passed back a fake smile. Dad hugged me softly. I hugged back, *uninterested*. "We thought you'll be out with friends to celebrate." Shanaya exclaimed.

She knew I had no friends after-

Do they not know me? I took a long breath before laughing.

"I had plans for tomorrow, I was kinda tired today." I reasoned and took the champagne bottle from dad. He settled on the sofa and mom sat beside him. "Your house is so organized, I wish Shanu was as clean as you are!"

"Mom! I am messier because I'm a doctor!" *Yes, that's such a valid reason, little sister*. I giggled (*fake*) and kept the bottle on the table, sitting on the seat.

"Are you sure you want to take business? We always wanted our daughter to be a doctor like us?" Mom asked me as I packed my bags. "Yes mom, I'm leaving for Pune and it's final."

"Let her go, she anyway couldn't score more than 650 in the entrance, she cannot do MBBS!" Dad mocked me and I grabbed the suitcase tightly. I did not answer.

"Excuse me," I heard my phone and left to attend the call. Ah, an escape. "Hey,"

"Hello ma'am, sorry to disturb you." I heard my assistant say. "You're fine, tell me."

"Firstly, congratulations on the win. And secondly, Oberoi wants to see you this Thursday." I smirked. "That could be a win-win, isn't it!?"

"It would be!" She exclaimed happily. *Might hit a billion.*

"Tell them, I'll be there."

"Ma'am, you have a conference on the same day." She informed. "I'll manage, schedule it 15 minutes after the conference is over." I instructed. "Noted. Have a good night," she replied and I wished I had one.

"To you too," I wished and hung up the phone. Smiling, I went back to the hall and found my parents and Shanaya drinking champagne, celebrating.

Wasn't it my celebration? At least wait for that!

"We're so proud of you, Shanaya!" I heard mom say. I joined them and dad smiled wide. "Ki, Shanu just got a promotion in her hospital. She's going to be the head of the department! We're so happy!"

I can see the happiness, dad.

I smiled and hugged her, "Congratulations, little sister."

"Thank you!" She jumped happily. "If only she was married," Dad smiled, caressing her head and looking at me once. *I know. Okay. I know.*

The celebration went on, neither was I asked to drink, nor did I pick up the glass. It was their celebration, let them be. I just wondered, when were they going to leave because my book date waited.

I picked up their bags and put them in their rooms, quietly.

"Good night everyone," Shanaya shouted and went to her room. Mom and dad wished me a good night and left. I would have had one, if you guys didn't land here.

I went to my room, taking my book which wasn't opened. Sorry honey, I promise to pick you up as soon as they leave.

I was alone in this family, if you can call them a family.

I typed an achievement note to myself on my laptop and fell down on the bed, tired of the day which was meant to be one of the best.

Chapter 4

KIARA

I went inside and sat on the table assigned to me. The business conference and party season was here and I hated to attend social events, but my job was to attend them. There was no other way to meet people and grab some clients.

It was boring. Hell boring. Before I could look anywhere else, a known face caught my attention as he sat right beside me.

“Morning, Ahuja!”

Black hair. Blue eyes. Cold demeanor.

“I cannot look at your face, ugh!” I grumbled and answered, for the first time in a long while.

And a wide smile- *what?*

“Is it so beautiful that you can’t even look at it?” Siddhant questioned with a smirk plastered on his face, *I wish I could wipe that off his godly face.*

An angelic face with all the devilish qualities, Siddhant Goenka was a self made billionaire and all I could feel for him is *hatred.*

"Will you stop talking Goenka?" I rolled my eyes at him and looked ahead at the conference. No wonder, he is back to his job of irritating me, that he left the VIP chairs for him and sat here with me. "I didn't even start talking yet, Strawberry," *that name!* He called me by that name again. Three years, I cannot bear this man around me.

Why is he back to talking to me? Didn't we agree on ghosting each other forever after that farewell happened?

Chiseled jaw. Godly face. Vinegar smell.

Even if I want to, I cannot get rid of this man. He is expected to attend all the business ventures I am supposed to. I wonder if I haven't changed my business plans by now.

But why is he talking to me today? There's something wrong with my life suddenly.

Mom. Dad. Shanaya. AND NOW SIDDHANT.

I looked ahead, ignoring him and his body. The only good thing he has, *that body*. The conference was boring, but a million times better than talking to Siddhant Goenka. I could feel him staring at something, it wasn't me, but something next to me. I shrugged it off and focused on the not-so-interesting conference in front of me.

"How are you even listening to this?" I heard him murmur again and looked at him disinterested. He rolled his eyes and I saw his file with some doodles inside.

And they call this man a genius.

I schooled my thoughts and didn't look at him till the end. I got up and was about to leave when I heard the same deep voice again, "Whatever-" I turned to look at him but he was talking to Aryan.

Brown hair. Hazel eyes. Handsome face.

Another angelic creation of god, Aryan Sharma was a famous author. He was popular among girls for creating one of the best fictional characters. I loved his book, "Soulmates" too. I am still astonished that these two are best friends. I don't know how Aryan manages to be around Siddhant.

He wasn't talking to me, so I quickly turned back and left the conference hall. *This man is a menace.*

How did he reach here before me? I assume I left the hall before him! Oh, I met Oberoi there. I managed to not look into his direction again, but he noticed me before I could leave. Leaving his McLaren's gate open, he came towards me with an expressionless face.

I hate him so much.

"See you again, Strawberry!" He gave me a small smile and went back to his car. I rolled my eyes and sat inside my car. He waited for me to leave, his eyes directed.

I rolled my eyes, *stop behaving like a gentleman because you're not, Goenka!* I started my car and drove outside the parking lot.

Ugh no way! NO FUCKING WAY!

My car stopped suddenly, I punched my steering wheel, frustrated. I heard the screeching sound of the other car's brakes and sighed heavily.

I got out of my car to look if it was fine. I love my Audi R8, who cares what happened to his McLaren. I ignored when he came near me.

"If you want to kill me just give me a smile, I'll die happily after that." Siddhant just what-

What the hell. Did Siddhant Goenka use a pickup line? GOD.

I looked at him wide-eyed while a shadow crossed his eyes. "Goenka, I came to check if my car was fine. I really don't care what happens to you and your McLaren."

Not the car.

"Oh no Strawberry, I think you do care." Siddhant and his delusional world. I rolled my eyes again and sat in my car, trying to start it again. *I don't want to be strangled here, I have a bloody meeting in 10 minutes.*

"Is there any problem?" He asked on the window, bowing to its height. *This 6 foot 1 bastard.*

I shook my head and came out of the car. "No, and you can be happy if I am stuck here. Now leave."

"Why do you think you being stuck here makes me happy? You stuck with me will be a little more delightful." I looked up in the air, he controlled his laughter. *Can this man ever change?* "Will you just leave?" I whined.

"I might offer you a ride, if you're sweet."

Him. Taking a favor from Siddhant Goenka, would be the last thing I would do.

"No, I don't need your favors." I denied immediately. "Come on, Ahuja. You have to attend a meeting." How did he know about the meeting? Is he following me?

"No I am not following you, you have a meeting with Mr. Oberoi, I met him in the corridor a moment ago."

Oh-

I nodded out of reflex. "So you agree to go with me?"

"No-" I replied quickly. "Alright, take my car."

"I am not taking favors from you Goenka, and this would be a HELP, too much." I replied sarcastically while he shrugged.

"Sit inside the car," It looked more like an order and nobody in the world orders Kiara Ahuja. "Add a requesting tone and a syllable called please, might help." I smiled and he groaned.

He was helping me, yet had to plead. Irritating this guy is fun, *since always*.

"Sit inside the car, so that I can help you reach your meeting on time, please." Why is he so interested in the meeting? Something's fishy, huh!

I rolled my eyes and sat inside the car. *What a beauty*.

He followed me and sat inside, driving towards the Oberoi's.

He opened his phone and typed something on the texts, keeping it back. His eyes never left the road, what and how did he type?

DON'T THINK ABOUT THIS GUY TOO MUCH.

I scolded myself again and focused on the road, trying to distract myself from his veiny arms, he shouldn't have rolled his sleeves up. Ugh, focus Kiara!

In no time, we reached the Oberois and I got out. Before I could leave, he stopped me. "Just like me, use a grateful tone and two syllables called thank and you." He smirked and I rolled my eyes.

"In your dreams," I passed a sarcastic smile.

"In my bed, maybe." I glared at him, while he sat inside his car and left. I shook my head and sighed, checking myself once.

A FAVOR from Siddhant Goenka, no wonder what worse could happen.

Chapter 5

SIDDHANT

Chocolate hair. Green eyes. Velvet scent.

Kiara Ahuja, the millionaire. She's best at what she does, either at business or at being sarcastic with me. She hates me so much, and it's funny, because she's given me all the reasons to do the same. She hates me so much, but I love that too.

I love her attention, even if she's not happy to give it. I'll love her attention, even after she hates to give it. *I hate her so much that I should be the only one having her hate.*

I looked at her going inside the Oberoi's and quickly went outside. My driver stood there, in her Audi R8, I nodded at him once, and he went inside the Oberoi's parking lot to keep her car, all in a working condition.

I drove back to my house, and I knew there was a problem inside.

"Welcome back, lover boy!" I heard my best friend squeal. He was having a bottle of whiskey in his hands and the problem was indeed big. “I am not a lover.” I answered and sat on the couch.

He laughed and sat in front of me. “Look at you, chill,” he hollered again and I need earbuds now. I imitated closing my ears and he threw a book at me. I caught it before it could hit me.

“I'll freshen up.”

“Hey, your best friend just did a favor for you and you didn’t even thank him?” *This man is going to shout this for my whole life now.*

“Your best friend just got into Kiara Ahuja’s car and worked with wires so well that it stopped exactly inside the parking lot. Now that’s some genius brain.” He raised his collars, imaginary to be specific. I rolled my eyes.

It was surely a genius brain.

“How is work?” I changed the topic, which worked. “Work is amazing, the director is final. My budget is big enough to hire the best.”

“You mean, my budget...” I looked sarcastically. “Oh baby, what’s yours, is mine. What’s mine is mine too-because you’re mine.” I choked on air. “Give him something, quick.” I ordered and went to my room.

Kiara loves this body, there are no chances she doesn’t. *I smirked thinking about her, she’s going to get the shock of her life.*

I bathed and went out wearing a simple tee and track pants. Aryan was sleeping on the couch, I shook my head at him and went to the dining table. Stuffing a bread, I opened my mac and started working on the new project.

I was working for three hours when Aryan woke up. He rubbed his eyes like a kid. This boy was a *kid.* I denied reading the book he was adapting for a movie, but I had started reading it secretly.

I wouldn't let him know, the book had a generous male lead and it was the kind of guy Ahuja would prefer.

Ahuja, where did she come from?

I shook my head and continued working. Aryan came and sat on the chair beside mine. "Why did you drink?"

"My best friend's lady sat on the seat of the car where he never let me sit, I needed celebration, Siddy and-"

"Don't call me that!" I hissed even before he could complete. "Siddy is irritated, well I have another news which can make you happy maybe."

I looked at him, he grinned. His lopsided smile showed mischief clearly. "What do you want?"

"Just a billiards game with you," he said quickly and I sighed. *I know the news. I can find what it is.* But a game with Aryan is not a bad idea. "Spit-"

"Aww poor Siddy, after the game." He got up and left. I shook my head and followed.

I picked up the stick, while he smirked at me. "You clearly enjoy the time with me, don't you?"

I do but I would NEVER say it.

"No, you're a pain in ass."

"Oh come on, Sid. You can easily find the piece of information I had, hacking my stuff or blackmailing me. But here you are, playing billiards with me." *Am I caught? Who cares!*

"Focus on playing Aryan, or you'll loose real easy." I pushed the ball and it went inside like a bullet. *Flawless.*

Aryan smiled and continued playing. I know the news he wants to say, I knew it before he would talk about it. But here I am.

Aunt and Uncle Sharma have been like my parents after my parents died. I have no regrets, because my father was a drunkard and my mother never cared about me. The only definition of parents I know were Sharma uncle and aunty. And Aryan, he has seen me grow. From class 2 to age 26, he knows me head to toe.

"How are your parents? Are they coming to see you anytime?" I asked, I really don't know how to have a conversation.

I speak less. I speak when needed.

Aryan smiled, pushing a ball. "They're fine, they miss you. We're going to see them in Delhi this Diwali, alright?" I nodded quickly. Who will not be excited to go and meet Uncle Sharma. He is a fun guy to be around. Aryan has got all his charms from him.

"Why don't you call them sometimes?" Aryan asked and I nodded again. "You'll nod your head off, one day!" He exclaimed and I nodded again.

I rolled another ball, the game was on a tie, "Will you tell me the information now?"

"Oh well, it's all over social media, the news is trending."

"The news of the Oberoi's?" I asked as if I didn't know the news. He nodded happily. *Oh I know you're a kid.* "Yeah, Mr. Oberoi has signed his new project with Kiara Ahuja, today."

I nodded coldly again. *I knew she'd get it. So proud of you, Strawberry.*

"Alright," I spoke as if I didn't care. "Congratulations, Goenka."

"I-" I tried to negotiate when he cut me off giggling. "I am going out for dinner with a pretty date, so I'll see you later." He left putting the last ball in. The game ended on a tie.

Finishing the dinner, after completing some work, I went to the file still intact on the table since Monday.

OBEROI'S

I smirked and opened the contract. Little did *my* Strawberry know what she got herself into.

See you again, Ahuja. I remembered my words from the morning and smiled softly.

Chapter 6

KIARA

I reached home, if you can call that place a home to live in, until my parents were here. I went inside, ignoring the disappointed eyes present there, I knew they had the same *you're late again* ready for me.

Little did I care.

When are they leaving?

I went inside, stripped and entered the shower, I was happy. The deal with Oberoi's was good, and about them working with me, it was going to be easy. I was excited, this is a big project, and I would have been a little too burdened to do it alone. I am fine with him or anyone from his company working as a partner. Oberoi's are experienced, and would be an asset too.

I freshened up and went outside. My so-called parents and their lovely daughter waited for me.

Ugh, I thought they'll eat and leave. God! When are they going back?

I smiled and sat down on the chair near my sister.

"Shanaya, did you check what your dearest elder sister did today?" My mom asked her favorite child. I answered, before she could, "Let me tell you myself, I met your dearest wannabe potential son-in-law and didn't act nice. And if it concerns you, I got a deal with Oberoi's which is going to be a big one."

I smiled and took a bite. They rolled their eyes, *dearest wannabe potential son-in-law,* I wish that egoistic villain was here to hear me call him that. My parents loved Siddhant, *for Shanaya.*

"When will you start listening to us Kiara?"

"I am sorry, dad." I smiled, I was eating as quickly as possible. I didn't feel like sitting here for even a second more. "Just a sorry and then going back to be the same." My mom taunted me. I ignored it and kept eating.

"Dad, I have a meeting with Oberoi's, I'll see you guys, I have to prepare." I nodded with a smile and left the room.

"She's so stubborn!" I heard my sister say. *I know I am, bitch.*

I went to my room and jumped on the bed. My eyes shined, I picked up *Better Than The Movies* by Lynn Painter. This has been on my TBR since forever and I finally found time to read it. I love reading, and the fact that my favorite color is red, so is my choice in fictional men.

Red flags are hot.

Wes Bennet was a good guy, as much as I read. I started to read, I put on an alarm. I don't want to leave this book unread but I have a freaking important meeting to attend tomorrow with my new partner in business.

Oberoi's. That old man has a lot of experience, will he work on this project or somebody from his team? Well, I think I should focus on myself.

Sometimes I wish I was in a book. To live a life there, to find a fictional boyfriend. *A life where a billionaire is in love with me and stands behind me when I burn the world.*

Haha no, I don't need somebody who burns the world for me. I want to be the one burning it, he just needs to give me the match. I rolled my eyes at my wishes, as if I would ever be able to. It is a myth.

The alarm rang in some four chapters, as much as I hate leaving an enemies-to-lovers in the middle, I have the meeting, or maybe, fuck the meeting. I started reading more and saw how Wes helped Liz out of nowhere.

Why did Siddhant help me today?

I suddenly closed the book. I cannot sleep with a question like that. My car was parked right at the Oberoi's office and I am sure it was him. Why was he being nice? *To annoy me?*

For my attention? Oh, right. Definitely for that. That cold blue eyed villain can never be nice. He must be laughing at his place after annoying me like that.

"Hey, Siddhant, and you are?"

I rolled my eyes and left. But those blue orbs were too impossible to not get lost in them. I went to the desk allotted to me and started working.

I should not think about him before sleeping!

Jesus, think about better things, CHRISTIAN HARPER!

Morally

Grey

~~*Men*~~

Fictional Men.

I shrugged and lied down, I knew I'll be overworked, but damn books over work.

I knew reading would get me late. I quickly rushed outside my room to the dining table. Stuffing my mouth with an apple, I was about to run away when I heard heels click.

Not again.

"Where are you going?" My sister's steep voice entered my ears. "I am afraid I am un-answerable to you, Shanaya."

"Are you going to meet Siddhant, again?" *Why do we have to talk about him?* I need to change my career choices of the past.

Give me a damn time machine. Either I'll kill this bastard or change my internship plans.

Internship plans. The life sucking plans.

"No, I have a meeting with Oberoi's and that'll be the whole day." She nodded almost immediately and left.

What is wrong with her? Crossing the dining table, I reached the hall, where my mom stood in scrubs. "Are you working here?"

"Yeah, by the time we're here, your dad suggested helping." She answered, sighing. It looked like she was on a night shift. "Take some rest," I was reluctant but it's okay to talk nice, isn't it?

She nodded, "I will."

"See you at dinner." I quickly left.

A civil conversation with mom, good start of the day.

I drove my car quickly to the Oberoi's. I hate being late, and just reaching in time. Reaching the floor, I had to be present, I waited. I was greeted by the manager, "Good morning, Ms. Ahuja, you can take your seat in the conference room. Mr. Oberoi will be there with your partner in business in 10."

"Alright, that'll be great." I smiled and went inside. I opened the files, looking around the conference room. The room was dimly lit, since there was nobody. The architecture looked just fine, I didn't check who was working with Mr. Oberoi earlier. The interiors were well designed.

Oberoi's had taken a leap, they were big, almost close to a billion. This project, if successful, would be their biggest leap. Mine? Well, I'll be huge too. At around the informed time, I heard the gate open. Mr. Oberoi came inside, and somebody followed.

Black hair. Blue eyes. That damned vinegar scent.

SIDDHANT GOENKA.

SIDDHANT ~~FUCKING~~ GOENKA.

No way.

He is not the partner.

He is not the one Oberoi's were talking about.

NO.

I prayed till I heard, "Ahuja, meet your new partner in business. Siddhant." He introduced us informally, as he knew we knew each other. I was surprised, this was *not* expected. Why would Goenka join hands with him?

Business. Growth. Big Deals.

I can't deny the six months contract, why did I sign that!

Work with Siddhant Goenka, ***God bless me.***

Chapter 7

KIARA

I looked at him as he sat right in front of me. My eyes are shouting loudly, 'CAN I PLEASE KILL YOU?'

He passed a small smile before looking at Mr. Oberoi. "I'm so glad to have you both on board. Kiara, thank you for accepting this offer. It would have been difficult to convince Siddhant otherwise." Mr. Oberoi thanked me. I nodded with a grin at him and preferred not to turn towards Siddhant. "Let's do a press-conference to officially announce the agreement, what do you think?"

"I would say, Mr. Oberoi, let's just announce it as a statement from our officials." Siddhant suggested and I sighed. Mr. Oberoi didn't look very convinced of his idea, unlike me. "No, I really think we should hold a small party, it is a big deal."

"Ah, that'll be-" Before Siddhant could continue, I cut him off. "Okay, it'll be okay." I answered. He passed me a known look which I ignored. If this man doesn't want a party, I definitely want a party.

"Excuse me," Mr. Oberoi got a call and he left the room. Must be important enough. Siddhant glanced at me, before looking back at his phone. I opened the files and checked if there was any loophole out of this agreement. I was not going to work with this man.

"Finding inadequacy in my contract, Ahuja?" My lips sealed into a line as I gave him a look. "Can you just shut up?" I asked, extra-sweetness dripping from my voice. "You plan on making me?" I punched the files and sat down, huffing. He sighed and stood up, bending down on the table, his face dangerously close to mine, "Strawberry, you're not finding an let-out clause in this contract. Let's just be professional enough, can we, darling?"

I gulped as he said that. His pupils dilated towards my lips and my breath stopped. He smirked at the reaction my body gave and sat back on his seat. I left the breath I was holding and looked away. There was something wrong with me today, or the thing inside my stomach and the hot feeling was rare. I blamed it on the smut I read in the morning and closed my eyes.

"On the scale of one to a hundred, how much do you wish me to kiss you, Strawberry?" He whispered.

I looked at him and beseeched, "Negative infinite. Or maybe, a hundred if we talk about how much I wish to kill you."

He smiled as he switched his seats next to mine and pulled my seat closer, "How about you tell me now?" Again, his blue eyes pinning me to the wall behind. My legs felt heat, and I knew I would dangerously lose this one. "Who talked about being professional a minute ago?" I mocked against his lips and he brushed his lips over mine before pulling away. *Ugh.*

"You love being that difficult,"

"I am only difficult around you." I groaned and he looked at me again. "So you're something just around me, interesting." He smiled getting up and left the conference room. I punched on the table again before standing up. "I am so sorry, I have a personal emergency," Mr. Oberoi came inside and told me. "It's alright, put an official statement, I guess." I nodded and left the place.

I needed a bath. I skipped going back to my office and reached home. My family was out, *thank gods.* I texted my assistant that I won't be going back today.

I shook my head, dismissing the unholy images that had suddenly crept into my head. I quickly grabbed a towel and entered the shower.

As much as I deny it, that moment was enough for me to imagine that beautiful face as if carved by Michelangelo himself kissing me. I couldn't stop thinking about his hands touching every place of my body, I'd never allowed anyone else. As much as I wanted to ignore the feelings that returned after three years of me avoiding them, they came back with a load.

A shudder ran through my naked body as I stood under the cold shower, water sharply hitting as it poured down my body. Despite the cold water, I could still feel my legs warm, particularly my lower body hot and numb. I desperately needed a touch.

I felt warm air fill me as my chest heaved up and down. *The shower head, fuck it.* My hands trembled as I reached for the shower head, the hot burning intensity that I felt turned my legs into jelly. My thighs were shivering as I struggled to stand straight. I placed my hand on the knob for support, lifting my leg before resting it over the water tap. The glass door of my bathroom had a foggy cloud due to my deep breaths. I tightened my grip on the knob, my knuckles turning white as I turned on the shower head.

Adjusting the water flow on the shower head, I carefully adjusted the jet nozzle over my glistening, warm and *wet* clit. The jet sprayed through the wet nerves, a gasp eliminating through me as I lunged forward. A sudden jolt of adrenaline surged through me, the contact sending a sensation of pleasure. The water went sharp on my muscles, *but delightful.*

"Fuck-" I whispered, deep gasps heavied through my chest as water hit the perfect spot. Loud moans elicited through my mouth, my eyes rolled back as immense gratification seeped in and out of my body.

Loosening my hold on the shower spray, my hand found its way to my *beyond wet* muscles, putting pressure on my clit. I rubbed hard and my fingers worked their way down my needed-to-aid area. Eventually, I reached the pinnacle of my high, my breaths steadied and so did my body. I closed my eyes and rested against the glass door, my back feeling hot and wet.

Feeling sore, I cleaned myself with the help of a towel before walking out of the washroom. I wore a silk short whose fabric felt cold and comfortable against my thighs providing relief. Before I knew it, I jumped on my bed and slipped into a deep slumber.

Chapter 8

SIDDHANT

I was getting ready for another business party. The month of social parties was here and all I needed to do was to wear some coats and attend them. Neither did I want to meet anyone, nor did I want any business from there.

Do I now? Yes.

My gorgeous business partner was attending this party since the host was one of the oldest shareholders of her company. She wasn't a social maniac, but she attended all the parties to meet new businessmen. I could not deny that her charms worked, and she had snatched away quite a few potential partners. But my worries had settled down, since those men didn't matter to me much, *fortunately or unfortunately*, she did.

I wore a dark green suit coat with a black shirt inside. I always dress formally for such business events, tonight was a little special one. I went outside to find Aryan, wearing a white shirt and pants. I raised my brows, and he looked at me with a grin.

"How do I look?"

"Fine, now where?" I asked, picking up my watch. "With you," He answered, his tone casual as ever. "I didn't invite you."

"Come on, Goenka. You never take a date, at least take a friend." I rolled my eyes as he teased. "I'm coming and that's final." He announced going outside. I sighed and followed, *how much I wish to kill him sometimes*.

We entered the party and all faces turned towards us. Of course. That was a case of every place we went. It wasn't just the looks, but the charms of my best friend. *Best friend, don't say that to him.*

My heart was closed, let it be.

We met the host of the evening and Aryan went out to talk to other women there. He had a flamboyant personality, but everyone loved that about him. There was a reason, his books were the best sellers.

I was standing alone near the bar, which was the only task I did in these parties. I didn't feel social much, nor could I hold conversations more than a *nod*.

The grip on my glass slipped as I saw her.

Green eyes. Gorgeous dress. Chocolate straight hair.

If a beam of light could be woven into a strand, it would be her hair. Those chocolate curls, today, straightened according to the long gown dress she wore.

Exquisite. Elegant. Enticing.

I had a hundred or more adjectives defining her, but we'll keep it for the other days. *This woman could break my heart into a million more pieces and still the pieces could find their way to her.*

Strawberry. She knew my eyes were on her, as she looked towards me once. She went towards the host of the evening and chatted happily. I kept looking at her, until I felt another gaze moving towards her.

Sometimes I wish I could kill in the open.

I saw Rohan Oberoi walk towards her and smile. *Bastard father. Bastard son.* I looked away until I couldn't and looked back at them, talking. I could not hear what they said, but saw Aryan moving around there.

He looked at me and smirked, realizing I was looking in Kiara and Rohan's direction. I rolled my eyes while he started hearing what they said.

Sharma- You need to be here.

I sighed before gathering myself to not punch the hell out of the boy and went towards them. "Missed the other business partner, did we?" I joined in as she looked at me. Passing a glance beside me, she smiled at Aryan. *Pass a smile to me too, Strawberry.*

Sharma- Stop being jealous of me.

I groaned, this guy knew too much. I looked at Rohan who smiled at me, "Mr. Goenka, I wanted to meet you."

"I wish I could say that too," *spoilt brat,* I didn't add. He laughed and shook hands with me. *Gross, clean your right hand.*

"Hold your glass in your left hand, Mr. Oberoi." I heard Kiara suggest before I could. *Like minds, think alike.* I smiled and she went back to talk to Aryan.

"No, I really like your books." I heard as soon as I reached closer. "That's so sweet of you, and your favorite color?"

"Red, indeed." She chuckled and I shrugged my shoulders. Now, what did *that* mean? How did book discussion lead to color?

Sharma- Red flag guys, un-reading ass.

I felt intimidated. This is pure harassment. I ran my fingers through my hair in frustration as Kiara and Aryan giggled on their book discussion. I didn't speak when they discussed 'Soulmates' since I wasn't reading the book, *as much as Aryan knew*. The whole event was then converted into a book discussion, where Kiara and Aryan chatted. I felt like a third-wheel, but it was okay, since it was Aryan and not some other guy who wanted his skull to be beheaded.

"Kiara, would you like to dance?"

"No, I've to head back home. My social battery is dead", Kiara laughed as they hi-fived and she quickly tried finding a way outside. Aryan elbowed me to go behind so I nodded and went behind her. "How does Aryan manage to be around you and your cold ass?"

"Oh, well, that question is for me," *she started the conversation. She knows I cannot.* "I really think he deserves a raise."

"We're making his book into a movie, what big of a raise do you think I should give him?"

"Such a mean best friend."

"I am not mean, come on." I retorted immediately as she laughed at me. She was a little drunk, well, otherwise her cold behavior would have been intact. She quickly sat inside her car as I opened the door for her and nodded at her driver.

Three years, strawberry. I'd still want to leave you till your car. Why am I not able to stop this stabbing feeling as soon as I see a guy around you? And why do I feel like punching even my best friend, if he steals that beautiful smile of you, from me?

As much as I know you're going to break my heart ***again****, and yet it is ready to be broken* ***only by you****.*

<u>ARYAN</u>

I don't know how long I danced. I had left the event as soon as I pushed Sid to see off Kiara. I was a party animal and I loved the clubs here.

Authors are the best matchmakers. Haha I am proud of myself.

I went near the drink section when I heard someone crying. I looked around figuring out where that sound came from. Am I drunk?

Oh no, there it is.

Brown hair. Black eyes. Beautiful face.

A girl was crying and drinking shots. No wonder-

Is she heartbroken? I went closer to where she sat and found myself a seat there.

"Don't cry over someone who won't cry over you." I whispered, if she could hear my voice in this music. It felt like she wasn't heartbroken, I wish, because that face didn't deserve to cry. "She did. She did everything. She cried, she tried, she-" she paused and started crying again. *Was she crying over a woman?* Okay, it wasn't a boyfriend.

"Calm down," I pacified again. "Who the heck are you?"

"Well, handsome as fuck, you don't know me?" I asked, offended. I ain't that bad as an author, am I? *She's probably drunk.*

She didn't even know what she was doing, I sighed and smiled. "Dearest lady, please stop crying. And tell me what happened."

"Excuse me? Why will I tell you-" She got up and started rushing out of the club. *People get somebody to carry your ass out of the club.*

I went behind her as she reached outside. This was the best opportunity for any guy, so it wasn't safe.

"Listen, what is your name?"

"I won't tell anything to a stranger." I shook my head at her childishness. "Ms. 5 foot 3 with an attitude of 6 foot 1, please go to your home."

"I remember the way to my home, thank you." She rolled her eyes at me and started walking towards the road. I sighed and went to her again, "Do you have a vehicle?"

"Drunk people shouldn't drive." She replied innocently and I couldn't help but smile at that face.

She was different, she had something which others lacked. *Okay switch the author mode off.*

"Alright, let's go sit in my car then? Don't tell me your address, just tell the driver and he'll drop you." She nodded and I reached the car, I texted Sid to send a car since I would be drinking. "Please drop her, she'll tell you the directions."

She sat inside quietly and told the directions to her house. I tried talking to her until then. "Why were you crying?"

"My best friend is angry at me." She answered and pouted. I can't- *I just chuckled.*

I waited for her to continue the story but that never came. She just sat there quietly and only told me the directions.

"So? You can apologize right?"

"I don't know how, I don't even know what to do. She wouldn't even remember me!" She told me and I was confused. Wasn't she her best friend?

"Why would she not remember you?" I asked. "Because I haven't apologized for four years." I closed my eyes hearing her reason. Is this girl crying in the club today for a mistake she made four years ago. How does that work? Did she remember it today?

Am I wasting my club party for her? Why does this story seem interesting to me?

~~Because she is different.~~

Because I am a writer.

Before I could ask any further questions, we arrived at her house. I got out and opened the gate for her. She got out, taking my hand.

Ever so soft hands-

I quickly shut myself up and she went inside. "Hey, thank you!"

I smiled, she wasn't a bad human after all. I wish, her best friend forgives her.

I am tired too, let's go read a little and then sleep.

Sleep. Later. Read. First.

Ahuja relates to me. She told me how she loves romance novels and has read all my books too. It feels great, at least she read my book. Mr. Goenka wouldn't ever do that much.

I reached home, and jumped on my bed. Completing my daily chapters, I planned on sleeping.

Chapter 9

KIARA

“You feel like the biggest mistake I ever made.”

“Please, listen to me once.” I tried to pacify her, but she didn’t listen.

“Kiara, do not show me your face, ever again.” I heard her say and leave. She didn’t turn back.

“VERMA!” I shouted getting up. My breath shallow, my heart racing, it was a nightmare. I tapped my face, sweaty. I rushed for a bath.

Getting ready, I went outside. This year’s medical conference was in Mumbai, this week. Now I know why my parents came flying here. If I hadn’t won that day, Shanaya would have mocked the hell out of me. Thank God, thank you God.

“Kiara, since Shanaya is the lead of her department in her hospital now, she’ll also join us in the conference this time.”

"That's so great," I patted her back softly. She smiled and ate her pancake. I silently ate, they would be out for sometime now, at least. "Take care," I wished them and left.

I reached my office and started working. I saw my schedule and saw I had a meeting on the Oberoi project tomorrow and sighed.

Facing Siddhant again, that ~~six foot one blue eyed gorgeous man~~ bastard, again. Three years of trying to run away with it. Three years of not thinking about that moment. Three years of Ahuja Group.

I wish I could erase it from my memory. I wish I could stop finding somebody to blame for that day. I just wish-

"Excuse me ma'am, we're shortlisting your fashion designers for next year. Do you want to discuss?" I was pulled out of my thoughts when my assistant asked this question. *Fashion designing, another memory which could drown me.*

"No, just pick up the best. Do not worry about the contract." I answered. She hummed and showed me the file in her hand, "This one looks the best according to your fashion style, do you want me to go further?"

I looked at the company name on the file and stopped thinking. I gulped, "No, choose the next."

I don't want to face it again. I would never face *her* again. She does **not** deserve it.

I looked at the shares of my company as I got a notification. The shares had increased by 2%, this sudden? Well, whatever! I love it.

The best news of the day, maybe.

ARYAN

I was at the movie set, *my movie set*. Siddhant was putting in a lot of money for this movie, but that was his way of saying, *you're my best friend Aryan, I'd do it for you*. Because that jerkass never said it from his mouth. He was always an action person, otherwise the universe knows Siddhant Goenka never puts money in something with no double returns.

That is why they questioned his choices in the Oberoi's, little did they know the reason for him dealing with them.

It had been a week since I saw those black eyes, something I couldn't stop thinking about.

"Mr. Sharma, so glad you could be here." A young girl, who looked like the director, smiled at me. I smiled back, "I love it, you have actually made my book into reality."

"Of course not, I LOVE THE BOOK, all letters in capitals. I met Siddhant sir in his office. He didn't even know I wanted to be a director, but he just guessed it. He is an amazing man." She appreciated Sid and I grinned.

Siddhant has always been somebody who spoke the least, did the most. My parents always appreciated him, despite what his parents were.

Everyone has a bad story and two choices. One being picking the worst part of the story in you or understanding the story and choosing what good you could pick out of it. Siddhant, however, always chose the second one.

His only wish was, Kiara Ahuja, and it has always been her. And I'd do anything to get it true.

"Sir!" I heard the girl say. "I am sorry, what is your name?"

"Mira," She answered. "Beautiful name, what's my job for today?" I asked enthusiastically. She chimed in with equal excitement, "The costume designer for the movie, Siddhant sir said you're very particular about the clothing so I wanted you to see her portfolio yourself."

I nodded as she opened the file. The outfits of the girl matched well to the independent girl of my story. I loved the designs, they were meaningful and elegant. This one, this would be perfect.

"This one," I picked up the file and Mira smiled. "I loved this one too. Ms. Verma is already here, I'll go and call her."

I waited for Ms. Verma, who was finalized as the designer for our movie. Mira entered the cabin, as energetic as she was when I met her, I loved the girl's energy. She will surely work her best for my book.

"Mr. Sharma, this is Ms. Adhya Verma," She introduced as another figure entered the cabin. I couldn't take my eyes off.

Black eyes. Brown hair. Beautiful face.

It was her. It was the mystery innocent girl. I had planned on going to her place- ew, that would have been gross. I collected myself as soon as she came inside.

"Hi, sir." She greeted me formally. I nodded, "Hello, Ms. Verma. I really loved your designs for the book. They are perfect."

"Thank you so much, I am glad we will be working together." She smiled and answered.

Did she not know me? Or she didn't remember me again?

"I do not read a lot, to be honest, but I loved your book. I plan on reading more of your work." Adhya smiled and said. Her name was gorgeous, and I already knew the future lead lady's name for my story.

She was determined, and didn't have a single personal conversation for the whole meeting. Well, that was *attractive*, no wonder why. I smiled and waited until she remembered we already met.

<u>KIARA</u>

I entered the Oberoi's for the meeting. I was still not sure why Siddhant had taken up this project. He would control the whole meeting like always and I would want to kill myself to be present, that is what happened earlier also.

I don't care, but still do. I was always jealous of how genius he was, not practically.

I went inside the meeting room, and sat on my seat. Siddhant came inside, and looked at my face. My eyes wanted to kill him, my lips pressed in a thin line, and my hands on the table, knuckles white because I clutched it tightly.

He gave me a smile, I rolled my eyes at it. I hate being here right now, I am irritated. More than just irritated,

I am confused why he took this business. He was enormous enough to take this company away, then why?

If it is any sort of revenge on me, it is working, Goenka.

"Mr. Goenka, well, I'd give you some time to catch up with our discussion. My team will be here in 20 minutes." Mr. Oberoi informed him and I looked at him. *I'll die then be in this room with him.* He gave a known look, as if he knew I didn't want to be here.

Well of course, he does. I nodded at Mr. Oberoi and he left the meeting room.

"Why are you here?" I asked, with no interest. "For business," He answered, sitting. "You clearly know I'm not falling for this," I accused, tell me why you are here.

"Falling for me then?" My face suddenly flushed, as I looked at him wide-eyed. He is confusing me, why does he do that when he hates me. *He needs to hate me.* Like I do.

"Goenka, you better get to the point, I have a lot more business to do."

"Of course, Businesswoman of the Year, this big deal. I totally understand, Ahuja." I rolled my eyes again, shaking my head vigorously. I was pissed, and it was undeniably visible. He smiled and sat on the chair, opening his file.

"You can sit too," He suggested. "I wasn't going to ask you, spit now." I ordered. "Sit and take this file, what did I say of being professional here, yes darling?" He softly requested and I gulped. Same thing, he knows I will be conscious.

I sat on the chair, crossing my legs, my eyes fixed in his. I nodded coldly, trying hard. He passed me the file and I took it. Our fingers brushed, and I looked up into his eyes again. He smirked and I closed my eyes. He opened his documents and started reading.

Chapter 10

SIDDHANT

Kiara opened her file and started reading. She bit her lip-

How would they taste?

I looked away. I have to get to the cabin where all the bots are.

BOTS.

I am not here for business, Strawberry. I want you to grow, while I have my concerns here. I have to clear the mess Oberoi's are creating in the market. This man and his son are drowned into a lot of corruption which you have no idea about.

She was reading when I quickly pressed my phone's ringtone and got up. "Excuse me," I said professionally and went outside the room. I knew where I had to go.

Bots, bots, bots.

Oberoi Group has been using computer bots for their company's rise of shares. The computer technicians which conducted this experiment are under custody, but they won't utter his name, ever. I guessed it myself, because this group was the only one, growing too fast by this year. It was clearly something fishy. It was EASY.

I opened the cabin, I had already checked the location twice during my visit here.

You're so gone, Mr. Oberoi.

~~Your target was Kiara.~~

Nothing personal, nothing at all.

I was about to attach the virus I had developed-

"What the fuck is your motive-" I closed my eyes and sighed. I ignored her green eyes striking me like a bullet and clicked enter. She looked at me in shock and grabbed my hands.

Grabbed my hands.

Grabbed my hands.

Touched me.

I looked at her and she gave me a questioning look. I shrugged and clicked another button. Another hand grabbed my bicep and tried pulling me back. Her tiny hands tried hard to pull me back, but all went in vain. I hid the smile that was coming on my face seeing her effort.

Finishing my work, I loosened my body, and she pulled exactly at the same time making us both fall over. My reflexes were fast, I placed my hands swiftly on her waist and pinned her to the wall behind us. Her eyes closed, she opened her eyes realizing she didn't fall.

I looked into those green orbs.

Calm. Nervous. Elysian.

She gulped, realizing her surroundings. "What do you think you are here for and doing-" I heard footsteps and placed my hands on her mouth. Maybe she didn't realize someone was coming and bit my hand. "Strawberry-" I tried to whisper. "What are you-" She shouted when I saw a man entering the cabin.

I have to shut her up.

I pinned her to the wall, my hands pulling her back, and placed my lips on hers.

Delicious. Now I know why she loves to bite her lips. Soft lips like marshmallows, lips that felt softer than cotton touched on mine. Her eyes went wide, I bit her lower lip to make her come back to reality.

Her eyes closed, her body went weak, I could see her body melting on my hands. She gave in and kissed me. Our bodies were pushed together, against the wall. Her hands on my neck, her nails clutching inside my neck. I placed one hand of mine on her waist, another hand on her neck, rubbing it softly.

We were both hidden behind the gate which was opened by a man. He looked around and closed the gate.

~~*I wish he locked it too!*~~

I hope he didn't lock.

Realizing the voice, I could feel her breath inside me. My tongue swayed inside her mouth, she let me.

Lips together. Saliva mixed. Eyes locked.

I never had a kiss. I never had a relationship before, three years ago was the first and last time I met a woman and she was the one I had kissed. Her lips were the first I tasted, and GOD I don't want another.

She broke the kiss, breathless.

"Strawberry, please be quiet when I ask you to, or I have to taste these sweet lips every time you don't." I whispered against her lips, she looked into my eyes.

Green beautiful eyes.

I can't-

"Let's go sit in the meeting, I'll tell you everything after that." I picked her up with the hand wrapped around her waist as she looked at me in shock. *Light as a feather*. I placed her on her feet softly as we reached outside the meeting hall. Rubbing her lips softly, I went inside.

Let's work together now.

She came inside behind me and sat on her seat. Mr. Oberoi wasn't here yet. Not even punctual, *ugh*.

We waited for sometime, no one spoke. He entered and sat on his seat, his team following him. She was looking into her phone the entire time and looked up, her eyes meeting mine again.

I don't know what this kiss was going to do.

Drive me crazy?

Drive me crazy.

Fuck.

Suddenly, the hate subsided and my life felt like *heaven.*

Chapter 11

KIARA

WHAT THE FUCK-

Did I just kiss Siddhant?

Did I just kiss-

OH MY GOD.

Mr. Oberoi entered and sat inside. My eyes looked up from my phone to meet him again. I looked away instantly and focused on the Oberoi's.

Oberoi-

What was he doing in that cabin?

What were those clicks?

Was he attaching something to know all the details of the Group? Why would Sid do that?

He doesn't need to.

He is going to tell me-

Face him again?

His lips were rough... YOU NEED TO STOP THINKING ABOUT THAT KISS KIARA.

I focused on the file he gave me earlier and checked the main points. The things were explained properly in the content written and I couldn't help but praise his skills.

Siddhant is a genius. But I ain't sapiosexual. Why am I even trying to find such points? I need to calm my mind down, and focus on contributing well to this deal.

~~His hands on my waist!~~

I need to get over it.

~~It was arousing.~~

Okay I need some air. I got up quickly.

"Excuse me, I'll see you guys in a minute." I nodded at everyone and reached the gate. I could see his back towards the door, I looked at him. Before I could look at something different, his blue orbs met mine in the glass table in front of him. He smirked, while I quickly turned around and went outside.

My chest heaved with the situation. I took a deep breath, standing on the balcony.

What the actual fuck-

My first kiss can't be somebody I HATE.

"Oberoi's are working with bots." I turned around, hearing Goenka. What is he-

Wait, what?

"Oberoi is doing what-?" I asked quickly. He came nearer.

He leaned against the doorframe and sighed, "He is increasing the price of the shares of his company through computer bots. You remember the business share fiasco?" I nodded, completely trying to ignore his Adam's apple bobbing while he spoke and leaned on the door.

Those lips-

SHUT UP!

"Yes, so that fake shares increase, only Oberoi's has been growing rapidly since the financial months, exactly near the time of the fiasco. On researching further, I got to know it was him." What did I get myself into! The last deal of Oberoi's is going to be mine, ah it'll affect my shares.

Just when my shares increased to 3%! Why!

"I got into this deal... to expose him." He informed me. "Did you know I was signed up for this too?" He shook his head, it did look genuine. But he's a master of lies.

"I did not know, Kiara." He said my name.

My name felt alive-

My name felt its meaning.

"Umm... So what did you do? And what is going to be the result?" I asked, I was doubtful. My shares, my company, my work is my life. *He knows it too well, and I hate it.*

"You don't have to worry, that was a virus which is going to affect his bots and stop their run. And the shares will be transferred, not destroyed. They will be divided in a 80:20 ratio in our company."

Did he say 80:20? Is the 80th ratio for him or me?

"The 80th ratio is for you." He answered as if he understood my question. "Why are you doing this?" I asked reflexively. "I don't need these shares, my company is good." He explained, as if it wasn't a big deal. *Well yes, not for him.*

"But why wouldn't you love it? It is you who developed the virus, you do deserve your part." Why would he not take at least 40%? He created the virus. *Why would he do that for me?*

*Siddhant Goenka is being nice, and I **hate** it.*

He whispered something I couldn't hear and looked at him questioningly. "I'm taking my part, Strawberry, 20%"

"But you could've taken more of the shares-" I cut him off since I still couldn't digest the fact.

"The more of the shares is for the part that you have to complete this project," He reasoned, this project is huge, why not! I would do it, anyway. "With me," He completed and I paused. "With whom?" I looked at him to confirm when he sighed and stood back and came towards me.

"With Goenka Group." I paused, my breath stopped. Work with GOENKA GROUP.

Work with Goenka Group-

Work with *Siddhant Goenka.*

I need-

"I will do it." I affirmed and paused. *WHAT-*

Personal hate- YES.

Professional hate- No WAY.

Siddhant Goenka, Goenka Group was BIG.

I have to be professional, I have to think about my company. I have put in the effort to be where I am, and this can be my best deal.

"You'll do it?" He looked at me again, so I gave a professional nod and confirmed. "So shall we go back and act like we're working on the project, or you still have to think about what happened in the cabin-"

My first kiss.

MY FUCKING FIRST KISS HAPPENED.

I shook my head, gave an ignored look and went back. I could feel his smirk on my skin, ugh, him. We reached the meeting room where Oberoi and his team were present. He looked at us with a questioning face while Siddhant crossed me going in first.

"We had some disagreements on my part of the deal, so I just cleared them out to her. We can work ahead on the project. Next Saturday, works right?" He looked back at me and I looked at Mr. Oberoi, confirming with a small professional smile. He nodded and grinned. *Unprofessional motherfucking bastard.*

Now I know why my shares spiked suddenly, but I am elated. Siddhant went near my chair and pulled it out, *this isn't professional...*

He gave a look towards Mr. Oberoi and I rolled my eyes sitting on the chair. Come on, it doesn't even relate. He went and sat on his chair, with the team initiating the meeting.

"How many days will it take for the shares to be transferred?" I asked after Oberoi finished the meeting and left. "This project will take six months while the shares take two weeks, the shift has to be gradual or it'll be visible to the world." He answered, looking at his file and noting something down. "The 80% shares transfer to the Ahuja Group and 20% to the Goenka, then when the project gets over, what do you get?"

He looked up from his file towards me. I asked a valid question.

His eyes.

His blue eyes had an answer.

An unknown shadow crossed his eyes before he looked away. I couldn't figure anything out.

"I get to see Oberoi ruined."

"Do you have a personal enmity?" I asked curiously. He looked towards the file and exhaled. "Not really, I don't like cheaters in business."

"Fair enough," I agreed. "I still don't believe you said yes." He said suddenly. *Honestly, I don't believe that either*. "But anyway, I'll get an official contract ready." He didn't expect an answer, nor did I have one.

I just nodded and got up from my chair. Picking up my bag, I reached near the gate of the meeting room when Siddhant opened it for me.

"You don't have to be nice just because we're in business," I smiled, sarcastically (I meant it)

"Trust me, Strawberry, I am just being nice because we're in business." *Siddhant Goenka being nice, not a good sign.*

Chapter 12

SIDDHANT

Ahuja agreed to work with Goenka Group.

She agreed to work with ME.

Was it business?

It was business-

Maybe it was me?

I felt good, my mood was pretty good today. It had been a day that I had kissed.

I kissed Ahuja.

I kissed Kiara.

I kissed Strawberry.

She was cold, but she felt *hot* in my arms.

She was ignorant, but she *couldn't ignore* what I did to her.

She was hateful, but she couldn't *deny* my deal.

Is the reason hate? I don't believe it.

I quickly changed into a casual black tee and sat in the dining room, waiting for my dinner. "Tan tan tadan-" I closed my eyes.

Did Sharma decide to cook? NO WAY!

"Aryan, I asked you to never cook." I groaned. "Babe, I'm learning." He smiled. "I am not your babe." I rolled my eyes, he grinned and served me another thing which I knew would barely pass my throat. "Goenka, at least try," He requested and I shook my head. "Please, I swear it is nice." He nudged again and I sighed. This man will be the reason for the food poison I die. I took a spoonful and kept it in my mouth.

Death, was the next work.

I closed my eyes. Go and visit hell but do not try eating this. "Come on Goenka, it is not that bad, is it?"

He asked again. I used a bowl to throw it out. "Come on, Sharma, let's try it." I gave him a sarcastic look and stuffed it in his mouth. He took that in for a second and ran towards the sink to cough it out. For the first time this week, I laughed out loud. I couldn't control myself.

"What the fuck, was it this bad?" He shouted as he came back. I was still laughing. He groaned and drank some water. I quickly gulped down my juice and looked around to see if someone was there to cook for me. *Ah, I guess I have to cook for myself today.*

"Chill, I'll cook something," I offered. "OMG will you, great go on!" Aryan shouted. I went towards the kitchen in the casual black vest I wore. Taking an apron, I took out a pan.

.

I was cooking when I heard Aryan shouting. The pasta was almost done and I sought it for the last time and went near the gate picking up the pan to make him taste it when I bumped.

Chocolate hair. Green eyes. Velvet scent.

What is she doing here? I waited for her to react, but she just looked at me from top to bottom. I smirked.

"Were you planning on some kitchen make-out?" I whispered, making her come out of the trance and look at me. Our eyes met, she was shocked to see me like that. "Uh- hi." Some words finally slipped out of her mouth. "Kiara, there you are buddy."

Fuck you, Sharma.

I looked at him as he entered behind her. "The master of the house was in the mood of cooking. Welcome," Aryan did the formality, he practically lived here so he can. "Here," I passed her the fork and also the pan so that she could taste the pasta. She looked at the fork and me once, taking it. Putting some pasta in her mouth, Aryan and I waited for her reaction.

"Mmmm," She moaned in pleasure, and I already needed an escape. Aryan looked at me and rushed outside, winking and acting like he got a call. *Fucker*.

She opened her eyes with a smile and I was already lost in her face. "This is absolutely amazing-" She muttered while picking up another spoonful. I smirked, "That's just food and you're already making noises," She looked at me putting the pasta inside her mouth.

"I don't see you getting me make noises other than food, Goenka." That felt like a mock. Did she just-

"I'd like to see you try." I kept the pan with a swift movement on the slab and grabbed her wrist to pin her to the counters behind. Her eyes went wide and her body stiffened under my touch. I looked her into the eye and she held my collar pulling me closer and placing her lips on mine.

"Strawberry-"

"Uhm-" She whispered when I broke the kiss and slid my hands around her waist, pulling her closer. She wrapped her hands around my neck, softly. I went closer to her, placing my rough lips hungrily on her soft ones. I bit her lower lip, she opened her mouth and my tongue entered. My tongue gilded around her teeth, our lips moved in a sync.

I rubbed my hand on her neck, she took a breath from my mouth. Our salivas mixed and this wasn't a slow kiss. It was hunger, aggression, hate- maybe. I broke the kiss and my lips traveled down her neck, giving her wet kisses, nibbling like a starving man. *I could never have pasta my entire life, her lips could be my entire meal.* She sighed and moaned when I bit her collar bone. I smirked at the effect and heard footsteps again.

"Somebody is here," I whispered, pulling myself away. She looked into my eyes, some other emotions than hate. *Your emotions towards me are changing, Strawberry, make sure you don't change them to hate again.*

Aryan was still on the *call* and took the pan, "I'll save some for you, in the dining room." He asserted and left. I looked at her after he left. Her hair was loose and her neck had a mark. *Mine.*

She looked like a mess, *a gorgeous mess.*

"What were you trying to prove-" She whispered, her body still shuddering. "That I made you make noises, except for food."

"Shut up, Goenka,"

"Make me, Strawberry," I gave her a smile, taking out another pan. That pasta was not coming back.

"Do you need anything specific?" I asked. "Didn't know you're so nice to your guests." She moved around and turned back to look at me. "Just for my new partner in business." I smiled at her. She might get an heart-attack on seeing how much I was smiling. "What is wrong with you, where is my business rival?" I shrugged and finished my cooking. "If you're done, tell me."

"No I don't need anything, a cappuccino would be fine, I'll get that." She answered and picked up the coffee box and a cup.

Reaching the column of coffee, she took out one. *Yes, I have a coffee collection.* And now, I know her favorite too. "You have a good choice in coffee," She remarked and I removed my apron. "Thank you," I had nothing else to say. "Did we just have a civil conversation?" She asked, dramatically. *Menace.*

"What we just had, wasn't civil at all, darling. Let's go-" I didn't wait for her to answer and reached outside with another pan of pasta. She came behind and sat in front of Aryan. "Couldn't talk properly earlier, how did you plan to be here?"

"I came here because Mr. Oberoi called. He texted and called you as well, but you were obviously away from your phone. He told me, so I said alright." I nodded and ate my food. I passed her some of it and she took it happily. *Such a formal, 'no-I-do-not-need-anything' person.*

"I'll just get dressed." I left, after finishing my food. Aryan nodded while she ate slowly.

Kissed her for the second time in two days. What is wrong with us? Oberoi's have done the only good thing, to get me in this deal. I got dressed in formals and went outside. "Let's go," She nodded and we reached outside.

Chapter 13

KIARA

Siddhant Goenka.

In formals, hot.

In casuals, handsome (I have seen him rarely)

In apron, shirtless, *MEAL*.

I need to get this man out of my head, I wish from the business too but that's technically impossible. We reached the car and he looked at me.

"Are you here to pick me up, or shall I drive the lady?" I gulped, his deep voice might be the reason of deaths. I shook my head, opened the passenger door and pointed at it as he gave a small laugh.

That damned smile.

He sat inside and I went to my seat. He opened his phone and dialed Mr. Oberoi. "Hey, yeah, we'll be there in some time."

I drove towards the Oberoi's. It was quiet, I don't know if it was awkward or comfortable. He leaned against the seat and closed his eyes.

Don't do that-

I couldn't move my eyes off him. He was relaxing, while my body wasn't functioning well. Okay, I need to control my brain and my reader ass.

"Do you not want to kiss that neck and let us die?" He asked suddenly and I looked away instantly. I bit my lip, *what am I doing?* I need to stay away from Siddhant. He is my biggest competition, and the reason for my high anger issues, sometimes.

Also the reason for- shut up Kiara. I drove as quickly as possible as he just smiled which I noticed from the mirror, I didn't look at him again. I am not giving you too many chances of smirking at me, Goenka.

~~He looks hot while smirking.~~

GOD! No.

I stopped the car and he opened his eyes, getting up. He was quicker to open the gate for me, and passed me his hand.

Not the hand-

Not the gentleman gesture-

Stop harassing my brain, Sid!

I rolled my eyes and held the gate, coming out. *You're not being nice for nothing, for sure.* He shook his head, as if he knew how my brain worked and followed me.

"I am planning to host an official party a week or two later, to announce this project with three of us officially, what do you say?" I looked at Sid, he blinked and nodded. Earlier he didn't want this- how did his mind change?

"I have no problem with this." I affirmed. "Neither do I!" Siddhant answered. "You called us for that?" He asked next and Mr. Oberoi nodded. "Yeah, I thought it would be great asking in person,"

This man! Mr. Oberoi, *you want to die.*

The only thing Siddhant Goenka hates was- wasting time. I remember clearly, three years ago-

I hid my smile but Sid saw it. He rolled his eyes and Mr. Oberoi shrugged, leaving the room. I burst out laughing and felt his eyes stop at me. I raised my brows in question, "What happened?"

"You're laughing around me, that's new." He got up and lightly tapped on my head, leaving with a grin.

Question number 1, *what is wrong with him?*

Question number 2, *what is wrong with me?*

Question number 3, *what the fuck is happening?*

I opened my phone and saw the to-do. Business event at 11- oh fuck-

NO! Social parties are a big NO for me! I huffed and pouted.

"Strawberry-" He came inside again. *Why does he still call me that? Neither did I know the reason three years ago*. "I was calling for my car,"

"I'll drop you," I said without thinking. *Shit.*

He smirked again, "Are you being nice to me because I am your business partner?"

"Trust me, Goenka, I am just being nice because I am a nice person," I answered and went outside. He *obviously* followed. "Well I would like to return the favor." He said as soon as I started driving. I looked at him, "You obviously would be coming at 11 tonight, I will pick you up."

"Umm no, you don't need to. I am well capable of coming by myself." I denied the favor instantly. I cannot grow close to him. "I know, I still want to." I shook my head again at his plea and dropped him.

I wore a black dress which fitted me like my second skin and ended right on the lower thighs. With black rose studs, and open hair in loose curls, I think I looked good. I don't like carrying purses so I just picked up my phone and went outside.

There was my family, sitting with somebody in the hall.

Black hair. Blue eyes. Greek Godly handsome face.

What was Siddhant doing here? I told him I would be coming by myself. When will he start listening to me?

I don't want him near ~~Shanaya~~ my parents. UGH.

I reached near them and Siddhant turned towards me.

OH MY GOD.

I don't know if I could react for a second. That black shirt and that visible body from those three upper buttons opened.

Devilishly handsome.

I cannot breathe.

He got up and smiled at me. “Hey Ahuja, you didn’t tell them about the deal yet?”

“Umm, I didn’t see them after the evening.” I replied, he nodded quickly. “I see you two having a civil conversation, that’s a nice update.” Shanaya smiled, joining in. *She has a huge crush on him.* To be honest, just look at him right now, *who can resist*.

I can already feel something in my gut, *fuck you, Kiara.*

“Just because of business,” I smiled at my not-so-lovely sister and she gulped. Siddhant saw the exchange and his hand caressed my waist softly. *When did he place them there?*

“Mom, dad, we have an event to attend and he’s here to pick me up. I’ll see you guys,”

“We’re leaving for Delhi, you didn’t mention tonight’s event in your schedule.” Dad chastised and I bit my cheek. *Fuck.*

I should have remembered and never let him come here.

“I am sorry sir, I forced her to join me as business partners. She wouldn’t have missed your departure otherwise.” Siddhant apologized and I looked at him. *He never apologizes.*

Everyone in the room knew that was a lie. But why did he do that for me? *UGH stop messing with my brain you devil. You said you'd hate me forever. Hate me forever then!*

“Hope you folks have a safe journey.” I fake smiled and went outside, clearly indicating to him to join.

"Have a pleasant journey." He professionally nodded at them and came towards me. I opened the gate of his car before he could and sat inside. He sat following me and started the car. "Drained relation-?" He asked and I kept quiet. Even if I want to talk about this to somebody, he's definitely ~~not~~ the one.

"You look stunning," He complimented and I looked at him. "Don't you think you should at least smile for that?"

"Umm I am sorry, thank you." I realized and thanked him quickly. "Oh no no, can't see you apologizing." I rolled my eyes and smiled, looking outside. One hand on the steering, those rolled sleeves-

This is bookish language-

Can't believe these things could turn me on. I thought it was just the description in the story but-

Never been attracted to some fingers...

God I wish this night was shorter.

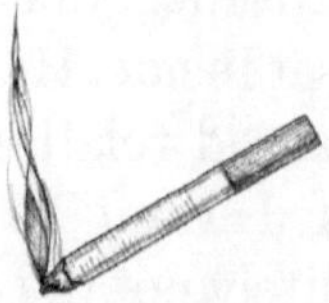

Chapter 14

SIDDHANT

Green eyes. Loose chocolate curls. Black dress.

This woman is going to be the death of me, and the world. We reached the event and she looked upset. Her relations with her parents are not what I thought they were. I've never been close to my parents, though neither did I see them after I could remember their faces, so anyway.

I knew she was upset and I opened the gate of the car. She silently came out and went inside.

That beautiful face had no confident smile.

I went behind her and she was standing with Mrs. Pereira. She was one of the meanest businessman's wives to exist. Mr. and Mrs. Pereira had been divorced and she took a lot of money away from the poor guy. Dear Strawberry, you need to stay away from mean people today.

I went closer to them. Mrs. Pereira mocked her, "You look a little chubby, eating a lot?"

"Yeah, eating with my own hard-earned money actually, that affects." *Woah woah woah!*

Strawberry was FIRE.

I controlled my laugh and gave a formal smile to the poker face. "Good evening ma'am, shall I borrow the beautiful lady for a moment." She smiled like she was happy with that and I knew she definitely was. Everyone who messed with Ahuja today, was dead. I smiled at Kiara who shrugged and went away, "Ahuja," I said as she looked at me like she'd kill me.

You're already my death today in black, Strawberry.

"Alright, I won't disturb you. Please have a seat." I made her sit and left. I finished my formality of meeting the hosts and went near the kids without letting anyone notice. I called a small girl near me, her eyes brown and she gave me a sunshiny smile.

"What is your name?"

"Lily," She smiled, answering. "You look smart," She complimented and I smiled. "And you look the prettiest, would you do me a favor?" I asked, with the max cute face I could make. She nodded quickly and I whispered something in her ears. She nodded and I gave her a pat on her head softly.

Lily went near Ahuja and she bent down her height and gave Lily that million dollar smile I was missing on her face. She agreed to go with Lily and the kids surrounded her quickly.

In the perfect place now.

I smiled and went to my corner.

Don't look there.

Don't look there.

I can't help it. I looked towards the kids and saw her giggling and playing with the kids. *She looked happy now*. I felt content and looked at everyone around, quickly sneaking out to go near them.

Shit. Don't tell her.

"Who told you about me?" Kiara asked Lily. "Smart man-" She answered and I sighed. Thank god I didn't tell her my name. I looked at them, they giggled at something soon after that and then she pointed towards the washroom. I went back, without disturbing them and sat on the dinner table. Ahuja didn't join for fifteen minutes and I was worried if she was fine. I quickly reached near the washroom but found nobody.

"GOENKA!" I heard a shout and turned back to find Kiara struggling to walk. *What in the world did she drink-* I closed my eyes and sighed, running to her. "Ahuja-"

"Yes, Goenka." She answered, laughing. "What did you drink?" I asked, hoping she'd at least tell me, if she remembered. "I don't know-" She answered and I grinned. *She looked adorable*.

"Why did you do that?" She asked suddenly when I took her to the nearest chair and made her sit. I raised my brows in question. "Why did you send Lily to me?"

"No way, I didn't." I stammered, how'd she know. "Come on, she clearly pointed you out in the crowd. I know only one blue eyed guy here. Why did you do that?"

"Because you were upset-" I answered and she pouted. "Now let's get you home."

"My parents will still be there for the next hour, I don't wanna go..." She requested like a kid and I smiled. This woman was a kid from inside. I smiled, and made my way towards the exit. "By then, let's get you something you like?"

"Yes yes yes," She jumped like a kid and I smiled again. I have never seen her so feminine, so gentle, so child-like or I would've adored her even more. I opened the gate for her and made her sit. I sat on my seat and started driving to her favorite ice-cream place, she told me three years ago.

I wish you'd never done that, baby. I wish you could have let me say things that day. I wish you had never avoided me. I wish you'd shown me you, then.

We reached there in no time and I got her the ice-creams, finding her sitting on the back seat.

Her legs relaxed, body loose, soft like a feather. I opened the back gate and she made space for me, with a relaxed smile on her face. I miss the old *us*.

"My parents have always thought of me as their useless child," She started and I just listened. She had never talked about her family before, no wonder it was alcohol. And I promise, it will be as safe as she is with me. "I was academically a low scorer as compared to my sister. And they just had to say that Shanaya was a better child for them. They wanted us to be doctors, I didn't want to be one. Shanaya chose that direction and cleared the entrance. I tried once, but I knew I didn't want to be. For years, in my own house, I was made to feel like an outsider, until I decided to choose to be one. I came to Pune after leaving Delhi and then internship, then Ahuja Group, and everything. I can't live with them, I know they're my parents but I just cannot-" She was at a loss of words by the end, so I quickly grabbed her and placed her on my lap softly.

She hugged me and hid her small body inside my overcoat. I rubbed her head, comforting her. "Now the ice-cream is melted, so we will get a new one." I said, kissing her forehead, after she calmed down. She looked at the ice-cream and grinned, "We will not waste this." She picked it up and dipped her fingers into the half melted stuff left in the cup and made me taste it.

"Melted chocolate feels, no?" She smiled again and I licked the ice-cream left off my lips. "Come on Goenka, don't you read books?"

I looked at her confused as she did the same thing again, this time getting up in my lap licking it off my lips herself, so seductively that I gulped. "See, that's fictional."

I pulled her closer to me in my lap, took some ice-cream on my mouth and kissed her, making her taste all of it. Breaking the kiss, I whispered against her lip, **"Is that how they do it in your books, strawberry?"**

"Mhm," She giggled and I got her another ice-cream. She finished that and looked at me with puppy eyes. "One more, tub?" I already saw her running out of the car, without her heels. Sighing, I followed and got her another tub. I picked her up till the car, since she wasn't wearing any shoes.

"You didn't tell me, did you just call the kids because I was upset?" She asked again. *No love, also because I couldn't see you upset.* "Yes," I answered and she giggled and bent herself more on the seat. I clicked on the button and she had more space to relax. *Perks of having the best car.*

"You have a great car," She complimented my car and I opened my phone. "What kind of a car do you like?"

"I like my Audi, but I wouldn't mind having a McLaren once I have those 80% shares," She ended with a childish wink and I laughed.

You're going to be the death of me, love.

I drove towards her home. Picking her up, I took her to her room. She had her arms wrapped around my neck, happy and relaxed. *Thank you, Strawberry, for being comfortable around me.* I reached her room and placed her on the bed, she reached out her hands towards me and pulled me too. "Do you wanna read?"

"You should sleep," I insisted but she shrugged and opened a book in her hand. She started reading and I just watched her.

I realized when she told me she can stay up all night to read, *she meant it.* Only alcohol can make her sleep now. I kept staring at how she giggled, kicked her feet in the air, hid her face in the book on the scenes, and my heart fluttered.

Better Than The Movies. Noted.

I wish this night was longer, because tomorrow, Strawberry would become Kiara Ahuja who hates me, again.

Chapter 15

KIARA

I groaned, my head hurting. I opened my eyes slowly, the room was darker than night. I sighed, maybe because I was sleeping-

Who did that?

What did I drink yesterday?

What happened at the event?

What did I do?

How did I even reach here?

I placed my hand on my head and pressed it, it hurted badly. The painkiller was right on the next table, *no wonder how,* again. I picked it up and gulped it quickly.

Did I sleep with somebody? Of course not, I would never let anyone enter my room. And I don't hook-up.

I saw *Better Than The Movies* kept on the bed, properly. If I slept while reading, that's impossible to be that neat. I groaned and rushed to the washroom, I needed a shower.

I came back from the shower, wrapping a towel around myself because I forgot my bathrobe. My head was a little better and I sat on my bed applying the lotion, until I felt I was not sitting on the bed, exactly. I jumped from my place and saw the last person I would expect on my bed. Looking at me, wrapped in a towel, which is slipping.

"Oh my god," released from my mouth as he closed his eyes and got up. "Ahuja, wear your clothes."

"What are you doing here, GET OUT OF MY ROOM." I screamed as he sprinted outside. I sat on my bed, sighing and wore my clothes softly.

Is that how they do it in your books, Strawberry?

I opened my eyes, they were wide-awake. I didn't remember things, but this line... what do I-

WHAT THE FUCK DID I DO LAST NIGHT?

I quickly wore my clothes and opened the gate, where he stood waiting, probably.

"What happened last night?"

"What?" He asked, cluelessly. I glared at him while he just entered the room and sat on the bed, picking up *Better Than The Movies*.

"Why are you here? What happened?"

"I am here because you asked me, and you got drunk." He answered shortly and I hate it. I will murder this guy one day. "What did we do? Don't tell me we did something when I was drunk, because you definitely look sober-"

He was quick enough to slide his arms around my waist and pin me to the shelf behind.

Fictional.

Fictional.

Pinned to a bookshelf.

I gulped but didn't break the stare. "It is too low of you to think of me as somebody who would take advantage of the drunk situation of a woman. I know you don't like me Strawberry but I wouldn't do anything like that to anyone, or you."

Fuck.

I shouldn't have said it like that. No no no-

"Anyways, there's breakfast on your table, have it and I'll see you at Oberoi's around three. Good morning, by the way." He said, picking up his phone and leaving. "Listen-" I shouted but he was gone. I pressed my head and jumped on the bed digging my face into the pillow.

Why am I sorry? Shut up Kiara you need to be sorry. Apologize to the devil, mentally noted. I reached Oberoi's a while later and entered the cabin they both sat in. Mr. Oberoi stood up seeing me, while Siddhant just looked at me. "Good morning, Ahuja." I nodded at him and settled on my seat. Opening my laptop, I started watching what presentation his staff presented. My eyes automatically moved towards Siddhant and he was watching the presentation noting things down.

He looked towards me, maybe feeling the gaze and raised his brows. I quickly passed the paper slip I had in my file. He glanced at the slip, then at me and opened it.

I am sorry. I didn't mean to say it this way. I was not blaming you, I had a major headache and it just came out.

PS- Swear to God tell me what happened.

His eyes went wide, *obviously*. I was apologizing. He looked at me and then started writing. Passing me the slip, he looked back at the presentation.

It's okay, Strawberry, any woman would think that.

PS- No, I won't tell you what happened. Trust me, we didn't have sex.

PSS- I feel like teenage college students, talking through chits in a classroom xD

I smiled at his reply.

Sigh.

We didn't have sex, but what actually happened. Maybe if I try, I might remember. I closed my eyes and tried pressurizing my brain to function, if it does.

Nevermind, it hurts.

I shook my head at myself and focused on the presentation again. The architecture looked very simple and bland. Though I know Goenka would point that out, I'd still note it down. *Do I know Sid that well?* I need to shift my head from him to work. And my curiosity too. I'll try remembering at home again, maybe that helps.

I noted more points till the end and quickly edited them on how to proceed. "So any changes you guys think we have to make?" Siddhant looked at me to start. Well, you have way more pointers than me-

I stood up and got the presentation slides I think needed improvement at. I showed them the bland part of their architecture and I also asked them to change the cash flow system. Siddhant followed me after I finished and told them more points to change, which I totally agreed on.

Personally, we clash.

Professionally, very similar.

I nodded as soon as the meeting was done and closed my file. I took the slip and kept it inside my bag, hoping nobody saw it. "No I did see it," I gasped as I heard the whisper near my ear and looked behind to find him standing. *Goenka, again.* I sighed, "Expected."

"Really? Great, now give that to me." He asked and I shook my head. "You anyway will throw it away..."

"No Strawberry," He slowly cut me off, his voice as deep as the feeling inside my stomach was. "I'll frame it, this is the first time you apologized to me!"

"Probably the last time, too." I rolled my eyes and passed the slip to him. He smirked and I shook my head, this guy was a problem. "Not the last time for sure, now where are you heading?"

"To Ahuja Group, why do you ask?"

"I needed to discuss the exposing plan. We can't talk here," He said looking around and I nodded. "We can go to the Goenka Group, you can sign the contract of our deal too." I looked at him, *he is a devil.* I still gave a light nod and went outside. "I'll be there at Goenka's in an hour."

"Alright, I'll see you there." He nodded and went to his McLaren. *I love that car!*

I quickly drove to the best food place in Mumbai and went inside. I was starving. The breakfast he served was a treat, but it had been hours to that. Plus, Oberoi's and their boring meetings.

I settled on my seat and the waiter came to me. "Is the beautiful lady waiting or would you like to order?"

"She was," I heard Goenka before I could answer him. "Good noon, Ahuja, what a coincidence." I looked at him, accusingly. "Yeah right," I faked a smile. "Can you excuse us for a minute?" He looked at the waiter who bowed and followed the instructions. Siddhant sat in front of me. "Sitting at two different tables won't be fun, will it?" He suggested and I already had another deal in my head. "You can sit here, only if you tell me what happened yesterday." I proposed and he smirked. "You're smart at times."

"I am always smart."

"Oh no no lady, I know it so well." He replied with a tint of sarcasm and I rolled my eyes at that. "You know what," I waited for him to continue, while I scrolled through what I had to order. "You need to stop rolling your eyes at such a heavenly sight."

"You? A heavenly sight?" I asked reflexively. He looked at me and I looked back at the menu, with a teasing smile. *I was sitting and having lunch with Siddhant Goenka, no wonder what was going to happen next.*

Chapter 16

SIDDHANT

Kiara looked at the menu with a teasing smile and I am thinking of ways to make her laugh. I only saw her laughing once with me, and Almighty knows, I know no sound and sight better than that.

“Now if you oblige me, can I order and hear what happened?” I quickly nodded and I knew she would be starving. The breakfast was light, since her head hurted. She called the waiter. “Umm, I’ll have a dabble burger and an espresso.” She ordered and then looked at me. “What would you eat?”

You.

“Same,” I answered as she looked at the waiter who nodded and left. “Yes and?”

“You just had ice-cream yesterday, after whining.” Her eyes went wide. “Then I took you to your bedroom and you kept complaining about how I was asking you to sleep when you wanted to read.” She pouted. “You explained to me the story, on the way you slept. You told me how you love romance novels so I kept them neatly on your bed. I had gone to get breakfast and then I was lying on the bed thinking that you're in the washroom, not bathing." She realized how she made expressions through the whole story and took her phone like a nonchalant kid whose lie was caught.

I controlled my smile, biting my lips as I drank water. *She was gorgeous.* "Okay, so I didn't do anything bad..."

"Oh not at all, and even if you did. Nothing you do would be bad to me." I replied as her eyes met mine again. She was flustered, clearly. She got a call and her face drained. I realized she was getting anxious so I got up. "I need to use the restroom, excuse me." She nodded and I left.

I went behind the gate and kept looking if she was fine while talking. I could easily figure out it was her family. She reads books, she loves books. I nodded to myself and went outside seeing her cut the call. I raised my brows to which she shook her head. The food arrived before we could talk so we started eating.

"Did I do anything else?" She asked out of nowhere. I took a sip of coffee and smiled softly. "No strawberry, do you remember anything?" I asked and smirked to which she shook her head quickly. "Nope, I don't think-"

"Just because you read, I wanted to ask if you have read Sharma's books?" I asked as she took a sip and nodded. "I've read the book being adapted to a movie, *Soulmates*, I didn't know you read-"

"No I don't," I replied and she made a face. "You don't do that, or you don't like it."

"Never tried," I answered honestly, lied about how I have been reading Soulmates and it was obsessive. She nodded, "The main lead of Soulmates, he was a businessman but when it went forward in the story-"

"Yeah, that mafia twist," I realized what I said and she smiled, a winning grin. "You don't have to hide that you read your best friend's book." I shook my head. "No, he told me that." I was reflexive and defensive, she cannot catch me that soon. She laughed.

She laughed.

That beautiful sound.

Those glistening green eyes.

She raised her brows and teased me, "Aryan would never tell this spoiler to anyone, ever." I just took my coffee and felt like drowning. She caught me way easily. "Alright, he pushed me to read his book. I was reluctant."

"But you couldn't deny your best friend, you love Aryan." She concluded and I shook my head. "No I don't, I hate that ass." She laughed again.

I was finding jokes-

Nevermind, she was still laughing.

We finished the food in no time, *yeah that was quick.* I wish I had more.

Reaching the Goenka's, I took her inside. We barely reached my cabin when I saw somebody arrive. "Kiara, how are you?" Aryan smiled as she shook hands with him. "I'm great, how are you?"

“Oh, handsome as always.” I shook my head. *Narcissist.* “Good noon, Mr. Goenka.” He bowed in front of me, Kiara just shrugged. “I have a professional meeting to do, if you can wait for a while.”

“Of course, anything for you babe.” He teased me. “I am not your babe,” I ran hands in my hair, he just looked at Kiara and winked. *I wish I could kill you. I wish you were not my best friend.*

I took her inside, opening the gate. She looked around the cabin. I was proud of my design, specifically for my cabin. It was a glass doored cabin with one side view glass walls, soundproof. The ceiling had a center cut with lights around. The shelves were arranged in a well mannered form and my table was perfectly cut into a crescent shape which gave my chair a bold boss look.

“This is phenomenal, Goenka. Your cabin is a treat to the architectural eyes.” She complimented and I just smiled. “Thank you,”

I went to my table and took the file. It was kept on the top, *priorities in work.* I passed it to her as she sat on the chair and started reading. Everything was properly written, there was nothing to hide anyways. I just wanted her to sign for six months with 80% of the Oberoi shares and it was already clear to her. She read the whole contract and signed it.

“Welcome to the business, Ahuja.” She nodded professionally. “You’re welcome to the Ahuja Group, Goenka.” *This conversation took a freaking three year time.* I passed her the copy of the contract which she kept in her bag. “The plan to expose?” She said and I nodded, sitting on my chair. “He’s hosting the party next week, which marks the ending of the two weeks we needed. I checked and the shares transfer is going faster than expected. It'll be complete by the date of the party." I told her and she nodded.

"That'll be perfect, can't wait to see him behind the bars."

"Ah, totally."

"Alright, I'll head back to my office now. I'll get my part of the presentation ready tomorrow." I nodded as she got up. We were about to head out when Aryan entered.

For the first time, perfect time.

"Kiara, are you leaving?"

"Umm yeah, the signing part was left."

"No way, you guys have a deal, secretly I know but, we know, let's celebrate." I looked at him. "Kiara, are you busy for the day?" He looked at Kiara. "Not really,"

"Then let's celebrate." Aryan suggested and I don't think anybody can deny Aryan Sharma for the party. "Where do we go then?" She asked, *she agreed.* I was about to deny it but now, well Sharma is my best friend anyway.

"Marquee, the best." He suggested and I nodded, sighing. "Alright, we'll go there by 11, you can rest and be there by then?" Aryan announced and went outside. "I'll pick you up," I told her and she looked at me again. "No,"

"I didn't ask you, Strawberry."

"You don't have to do that for a business partner-" I moved towards her, she moved back until she reached the glass window. "Baby, the next time you said we're business partners, I am afraid I might have to shut you up the way I did."

She knew I was serious. She bit her lip and slipped outside. I smiled, following her outside. I saw a guy eyeing her, "Goenka, I think I forgot my phone." I nodded as she went inside. I went closer to the boy, "Fired."

"Sir-"

"Look at her like that again and you'll be fired from every company in India." He gulped and started packing his things up. Kiara came out of the cabin and I followed her till her car. "I'll see you tonight." I saw her car leave and went inside. Aryan was smirking at me.

Chapter 17

KIARA

I reached home and went to my wardrobe. A party dress. Pulling out a number of dresses, I couldn't find something, there was something missing. AH! I don't have anything to wear.

Why would I say that?

I sighed and sat on the floor. I was confused, I was going out with Siddhant for the first time-

Siddhant? I was going to a party with Aryan. I found a dress which looked perfect for a club night.

~~Something somebody might not be able to resist.~~ I took it out and swiftly went for a shower.

.

Red is the color of danger, red is the color of emergency, red is the color of fire. I was all ready, dressed in a red bodycon. It was a sweetheart neck, slit at the waist dress, ending right below my inner thighs. With open loose wave curls, I wore a nude lip and a pencil heel.

Heels would be a problem. Little did I care.

Glancing myself once in the mirror, I moved outside. My mobile pinged and I opened the text.

Siddhant Goenka- I am outside.

I reached outside, he was waiting near his car and looked towards me. *I forgot to breathe.*

Dressed up in a casual black tee and denim, this guy could take any woman. I already felt something in my gut when he glanced at me, his eyes full of desire, something which we both knew.

Desires. Something which I have, but I'd still choose not to. I am not worth this guy. I am not worth the other emotions he has, except for the desires. "Let's go," I suggested as his glance shifted and he nodded, back to his cold demeanor. He opened the gate of the car, as always. I sat inside, he followed. His biceps were visible, his veiny hands. It was going to be a long night, *he looked so hot.*

I looked at myself in the mirror once we reached. "You look perfect, Strawberry. Let's go. And let me know if you need anything inside."

"You don't have to worry about me, I know how to manage." He shifted closer and looked at my hair.

"You're my responsibility," He tucked a strand of hair behind my ear and the amount of butterflies I had when his fingers brushed my skin, was close to infinite. He smirked at my body's reaction and went outside, opening the gate and passing his hands again. This time, my body didn't hear my brain, instead my heart, which was fluttering. My hands went in his and he pulled me out.

All eyes on him. Women were gawking at him and I couldn't help it. He looked like a Greek God. We went inside and saw Aryan waving at us. We moved towards the table when a guy came nearer, he looked drunk. Siddhant's hands grabbed my waist softly as he pulled me to another side and the man crossed him. *I looked at him, he was just looking further.* His hands lingered on my waist as we reached the table. Aryan gave me a side hug and I responded to it.

Aryan was a charmer. His hair and hazel eyes would be the best combination any woman would ever want. Plus his vocabulary, this man was Add-

What did I-

No.

I should stop thinking. This is definitely not the time to think about college. I glanced at Siddhant who was sitting and sipping his whiskey. I had chosen wine, the best option here. While Aryan, he was ready with the shots. "Ahuja, why don't you compete?" I smiled and shook my head as he suggested. "Come on, don't tell me you haven't ever tried." He implored again. "Oh I have, excuse me!" I acted fake- offended and laughed. Siddhant was just hearing our conversations. He speaks less, he speaks when required.

"So, let's do it." I couldn't deny him anymore and nodded, I wanted to have some fun. *Siddhant would manage, again.* I shook my head at my thoughts and just gave it. Tonight is the last night! Aryan got shot glasses for me as well and we both sat together. "Goenka, be the referee!" Aryan shouted and I giggled at the thought of Siddhant Goenka saying '1-2-3-Go!' to us. Siddhant gave me a 'I know what you thought' look and I laughed again. *Felt like three years ago.*

Shut up Kiara! Forget the memories for today and just ENJOY!

"Okay, I'll say it." I said and he was ready. "1-2-3-GO!" I screamed and we both started taking the shots. I was in a competition and I knew how to win. Aryan was very fast, indeed. But we both reached the last shot together, he took it in, while I was the one to finish first. *I don't know how that happened.* We both giggled by the end. Siddhant shook his head and I pulled his cheeks. *I am drunk.*

"You look cute!"

"I know right, he is!" Aryan shouted back at me and we hi-fived. Siddhant's eyes went wide at Aryan. They were best friends, ah. *My best friend-* I hiccuped and skipped the topic. Haha, drinking me is FUN!

I laughed again. "You two stay here, I will go dance." Aryan yelled and left. I looked at Siddhant who was just looking at me, ever so softly.

So this is what happened yesterday, he *watched* me? He watched me do silly things? I know I am not going to remember one word I am thinking about him right now, but do I care? NO BABY!

His green eyes full of emotions today- hate probably? Please keep hating me Sid, I am not worth it. "What happened, Goenka?"

"Strawberry, you're drunk again." I hiccuped and laughed. "So? Even Sharma drank?"

"He's resistant, he can drink more. You aren't." He scolded me like a father and I giggled again. "Stop being my dad, be daddy instead." I laughed at my own joke and ran to the dance floor. *Where did Aryan go?* I shrugged and started dancing. A man soon came along to dance with me, while I just turned around and moved. I did not face him.

Soon, I felt a pair of arms around my waist and I turned back to kick him back when I realized it was Siddhant. "You? You dance?" I asked as he twirled me around. "Only with you." I blushed hearing his reply. I couldn't help but giggle.

Okay, I am drunk and now something bookish happened to me. I want to kick my feet in the air and hide my face. I need to stop blushing. "Did you just blush?" I heard him looking at me, all flustered. *You won't get it babe. You would never.* "It was-" I smiled happily. He smiled softly and was about to pick me up... "NO!" I shouted. *Why am I doing all this?* I AM DRUNK YAY!

He looked at me questioningly and I grinned jumping on a chair, then on his back. His body was swift in carrying my legs, while I wrapped my arms around his neck, settling myself. *I was damn comfortable around this guy*. I have no idea why I could not keep my walls up around him. It was as difficult as being easy around my family. He took me to his car and made me sit inside. "Now sit like a good girl," He said softly.

He has a soft side. SIDDHANT HAS A FUCKING HEART. ***A heart that I adore,*** *but I'll forget tomorrow.*

I heard him call somebody, oh it was Aryan. “Sharma, I am taking Ahuja home. Take care of yourself, I’ll send a car.” He instructed Aryan and then sat inside to start driving.

He cared about Aryan. He cared about him a lot. I hope I remember everything tomorrow.

I felt drowsy and didn’t know when darkness occupied me.

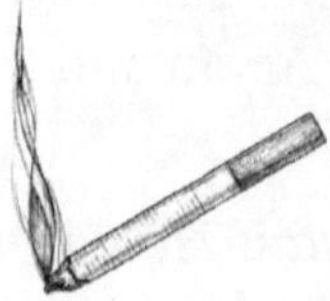

Chapter 18

SIDDHANT

I made Kiara sit inside the car and called Aryan. "Are you drunk?"

"No I am not," He laughed on the call, his voice clear, though the club had a lot of music. Maybe he wasn't on the dance floor. "Sharma, I am taking Ahuja home. Take care of yourself, I'll send a car." I instructed him on the phone. "You're a sweetheart."

"I am responsible." I retorted and he laughed again. I drove towards her house, making sure of the heater so that she doesn't get up. Kiara was curled up in a ball and was sleeping with a smile on her face. She looks cute while sleeping. *A perfect sight to look at.* I reached her place and took her inside, picking her up as softly as possible, so that she doesn't get up. I placed her on the bed, she snuggled into the blanket and kept my hand between hers. Sighing, I sat beside her.

"You look so cute!" I chuckled to myself. I wish she was herself around me. I wish she didn't bring her walls up

and behaved as if she hated me. I wish she knew she was *always mine to be* and I was always hers. All I knew was, I hope she doesn't forget this tomorrow. I was halfway sleeping when she shifted my hand closer and moved towards my lap. Her head was almost on my thighs as I sat and she slept soundly.

The peace she had on her face was the first time I had seen around me. The last time I'd seen it was *three years ago*. I wish I could erase that day and have her all to myself. I wish I wasn't heartbroken that day.

She woke up with a headache, again. As she groaned. I was a light sleeper and got up as soon as she shifted. Her hand was on my crotch and she realized it and pulled away quickly. I kept my eyes closed. She tried making sure I didn't open my eyes and ruffled my hair softly. It was not as bad as the day before and she went outside.

I opened my eyes and washed my face, before going downstairs. She was in the kitchen, and went and stood right behind her. "Strawberry, I would have volunteered for the breakfast."

"No more favors from you, Goenka." She hissed and I smiled. "Well, I am running late. I have a meeting to attend, so, have a good day, Strawberry." I wished and took the coffee from her hand. It was a mocha, and I was a black coffee drinker. I still took a full gulp of it and passed the cup back to her.

"You never liked mocha-" I looked back when she murmured. Coming back to her, I placed my fingers on her chin and made her look up at me. Pressing my lips into hers, I took the taste of chocolate she had on her lips, she didn't move a bit.

"Mi piace tutto quello che ti piace, fragola." I whispered to her in Italian and left. She will never understand, I am sure she doesn't remember what I said to her. I took a long warm bath, and got ready for the work I had to do today.

Today's work didn't involve Ahuja, and I already missed her. After a long time, I felt like skipping work. I went outside, when I saw Aryan puking. I rushed to him as he puked into the sink again. "What is wrong with you?"

"I- shut up bro how would I know?" He said between puking. I closed my eyes, and went outside to find the medicines. Passing one to him, I told him to sit inside the car. "I don't need a doctor,"

"Yes you do, shut up and let's go." I took him to the hospital and sat outside as he sat inside with the doctor, shooting me daggers through his eyes. I smiled and looked at my phone as it blinked with the name, Strawberry.

"Hello,"

"Where are you?" She asked straightforwardly. I sighed, "In the hospital, honey."

"Goenka, I have work," I saw her sigh, "I am serious," I emphasized. "What-?" Her reaction came out louder than usual. "You're hurt?" She asked. *Is she concerned? Is she affected?*

"No, Sharma has puked like a hundred times now." I was pissed off, taking care of Aryan-who-doesn't-listen-to-you-at-all-Sharma was a dangerous task. She laughed looking at me sulk. "Strawberry, don't you dare say that to anyone. I haven't come since the start, I just dropped by." She smirked, *I just sulked*. "You look cute while sulking,"

Did she just-

Did Kiara call me cute?

I looked at her with pleading eyes and she laughed. "I won't ask politely again," I grunted. "Maybe I like the impolite version," She winked. I raised my brows and she started coughing. *Fake coughing*. "I was kidding."

"Joking with me, progress number two, lady." She rolled her eyes. "And if you meant what you said, I have never been polite to you anyway." She looked into my eyes through the phone and didn't say a word. "I have a lot more things to do than have a small talk with you, Goenka." She found words, *basically a sarcastic comment*. Obviously. I smiled, "So, why did you call?"

"I need to know about the updates. How is the transfer going? Does Oberoi know anything yet?" I shrugged hearing all the questions she asked. "Transfer is 55% complete and we'll be ready before the party, for the party and the drama. Oberoi's know nothing, their reflection will be visible after it is done." I stopped talking. I don't know how to hold a conversation.

"You don't have to be concerned, you'll be free within a week."

"The deal with you is a six month project, no way I am free-" She retorted. "About that, you'll never be free." I looked up from the call, Aryan came outside. He went towards the washroom as I looked at her again.

"Goenka, as soon as the party is done, or maybe from now, let's go back to being professional. I will not forget what happened in the past." *The past*.

Eh. Why would she suddenly bring up the past in between? And she didn't forget?

It is ***me*** who shouldn't.

"Neither do I, Ahuja. But that doesn't change the fact that I still believe the same." *I still have the same feelings for you.* "Do you? Where were you in the three years?"

I had my ambitions. Just like you did. I chose to never come back until I found Oberoi's attacking you to win another deal. I chose to never give my heart another chance to be broken again. I chose to forget what you did three years ago and give us *another chance*. I chose to come back to you, you didn't even do that!

I didn't answer. I needn't answer. She didn't care, *neither before nor now*. She still thinks I'd be a problem to her career. She still hates me.

All she needs is to be told what is between us.

KIARA

I hated what I had felt after his vinegar smell had left the kitchen. I hated that I was weakening my walls around him. I hated him because he was still my business rival, his company was still my biggest obstacle to be number one.

I had reached the Ahuja Group in the morning since he had left. Being busy distracts you from a lot. And it was far better than to think about your business rival and feel something in your gut. *I wish I had never met him.* I wish I had known him differently.

Something inside me had changed for him. Three years ago, Kiara Ahuja would have still hated him after that day. But now, I knew there was no going back to where it was. *The hate*. How can it?

It can never be the same, his niceness, his business proposal, his help against Oberoi have got something changed in my head. And it was definitely not the physical attraction I was going to name it. It wasn't hate, maybe *dislike*.

I shrugged all my thoughts again and started working. *Where were you in these three years?* This question had a long answer, that he had, he could've chosen to blame me. He could've chosen to shout it on my face that it was my decision.

But didn't he react to my decision? Didn't he betray me worse than my decision to him? Didn't he choose to do that on the farewell day so that he proved he didn't care? Now if he chose that, I had one more chance to decide to never fall into the trap again. *I will never*.

I heard a knock on my cabin door, "Come in."

"Hey there, Ahuja." I sigh. He didn't have to come here. I was in no mood to face him right now. I rolled my eyes as he took the seat in front of me. "Do you want to go and shop for the party?"

"No." I looked at him once and went back to my laptop. I had nothing to do.

Chapter 19

SIDDHANT

“But Strawberry-”

“Call me with that name again and I am gonna shoot up. Be professional, Goenka.” She shot from her mouth. I looked at her, as she got up from her seat and came in front of the table. Resting against it, she passed me the same hateful glance she had.

What suddenly changed her mind? I got up, wrapping my arms around her and pulling her closer. Her face dangerously close to mine, I whispered against her lips, “So you don’t feel anything?”

“It’s a physical heat, that is possible with anyone.”

“Touch another man and he’ll only be the one burning, *literally*.” I intimated her, and I was serious.

“You don’t own me, Siddhant.” That fucking name from her mouth. That fucking whisper. I placed my mouth on her, grabbing her neck towards me. “We both know,

I do. Don't you remember, Strawberry?" I whispered between the kiss.

Lips fighting for dominance.

She is the only woman whose lips I have tasted and she'll be the only one. And if she thinks, by behaving like that, she can change the fact of how crazy I was about her three years ago, it won't. Her silk pants were smooth enough to be pushed away as I pushed my hands through them. Her mouth exhaled inside mine and she gasped as I reached her clit.

"You always wanted me to make you scream my name from the beautiful mouth of yours, didn't you?" I said as my fingers delicately moved inside and she moaned. *And she says she feels nothing. Her clit says something else.* Her hands were wrapped around my neck and her head fell back as my fingers thrusted inside.

She moaned louder and I moved my hands in a swift motion again to hear those screams. *Oh gorgeous she looked.*

I don't care if that cabin wasn't sound proof, the ears that hear her moan except me would hear no sound in future.

"Sid- oh my!" She screamed and I covered her mouth with my hand softly. "I wouldn't like you being heard by somebody, love." I said kissing her, my hands still in rhythm.

Slow and fast.

Round and round.

Thrust.

Thrust.

Thrust.

And she squeezed. She squeezed so hard, I felt my fingers break. She looked at me, clear in the eyes as I took out my fingers and licked them.

"***I call you strawberry, because you taste like it.***" I said, licking my fingers as she grabbed my collar and pulled me into a kiss again. I smiled, kissing her back. "You're a devil." She blamed.

"And I know you love villains." I whispered against her mouth as her phone rang.

She sighed before picking it up. "Yeah, no, I'll be there in ten." She looked at me, hanging up the phone. I fixed her dress softly.

"You tell me you hate me, love. But your screams when my fingers tease you don't say that. All I was here was to tell you, that *you know what it is between us*. Next time you talk about another man around you, **I'll show you how to make a man beg for life.**"

"Fuck you, Goenka."

"I know you want it desperately, love." She slipped away, glaring into my eyes. I quickly wrote a note for her and left.

Take care, love.

I'll see you at the party.

She feels. She feels every bit of it. But she doesn't want me to know, and *I hate to not know WHY*.

I did not meet Ahuja after that. I didn't text, neither received one. I was getting ready for the party at

Oberoi's. The day Oberoi was going to die. I didn't know why I didn't try through the whole week. Maybe because I wanted to give her the time to realize.

Maybe because I wanted to give her a chance to come to me.

Maybe because I wanted her to choose me.

Kiara was *it* for me. She was probably the one, even three years ago.

"Hey, Siddhant, and you are?" She didn't answer me.

Green eyes. Chocolate hair. Velvet scent.

I saw Kiara for the first time that day. It was my first day at an Internship in Pune. I was in the Conrad School of Business, my college was one of the top colleges in India. She didn't answer me and went towards her table.

Was she an intern too? Or did she belong to the company as an employee? I knew nothing but those green eyes were deep enough that I wanted to drown. I waited until another formally-dressed lady entered the block. "Good morning, students. Square one to square twenty seven, all of you are expected to work with all your brains and we expect good results from CSOB and Nationals."

I looked around to find her sitting on square twenty, my birthday, that's idiotic but whatever. But she was an intern like me. And she was from Nationals. She looked absolutely focused and determined to score the best in the internship. I was only here for experience and the degree required us to do one internship, at least.

"Kiara," I heard a girl from square seven say. I couldn't see who it was since the girl my eyes had focused on stood up on that name. So that was her name, Kiara.

Everyone sat together at lunch as CSOB met Nationals and they tried making friends. I wasn't a social person and I sat on the last chair in the corner, when I saw Kiara sit right beside me. "Not social?" She asked and I nodded. "Kiara Ahuja," She passed her hand and I shook it. "Siddhant Goenka."

"Are you working for the Goenka firm?" She asked, as if surprised that I was too young to work in a firm. Let's surprise her more, "I own that firm."

"It's- oh wow." She looked more surprised and I nodded. "You will nod your head one day, try smiling probably."

"Uh, that's the first time I've been told that." I answered and she chuckled. "Everyone's boring, what's your CGPA?"

"9.7" I answered and she looked at me shocked. "You don't look like a nerd, nerdy."

I shook my head defensively, "I am not a nerd,"

"Here," She passed me her box and it had chocolate muffins inside. I wasn't a sweet eater, but I picked up one. "Thanks." She gave me a grin and picked up another. "It'll be great working with you,"

"Likewise," She wished me back as the break ended and everyone went to their work squares.

I clearly remember what she wore on the first day. A red midi dress with tulip sleeves and I have adored her fashion choices since forever.

Our internship was for three months but it never felt like one. She was cheerful and friendly with everyone around while I was somebody who only spoke at meetings. We were very different, yet we were similar. Her smile wasn't real, her cheerfulness was until she had to socialize in a group.

The more I spent time with her, the more I wanted to know her. She hid a lot of things behind that gorgeous smile of hers, but she never told me as much as I tried.

We were close to the farewell party at the internship. Everyone had become really cordial and Kiara and I were appreciated for the work we had done. Kiara always told me she envied how genius I was with architecture and how she wanted to snatch position one from me. ***But what I didn't know, that she was serious.***

"Kiara, do you wanna go with me to the farewell?" I finally found the courage when we were a week away from our farewell. By now, I had understood her. By then, I knew she was a very strong, determined, career focused woman, who had nothing above her career.

She looked at me, and made a face, questioning. "Sid, you think I'd ever go out with my biggest competition here?"

"The competition here? I mean- that isn't even a-" I tried to reason before I was cut off. "No baby, of course not. Life is always a competition and I will always win."

Win it. Win your competition. At what cost, love?

"I never thought of it as a competition. I honestly don't even care what I do here. I am going to go back and work my ass off at Goenka Group." I told her, and she smiled. "Group, well, it's not a Group yet."

"Trust me, darling. One day, it'll be taking the best business award."

"I hope I get the businesswoman of the year in the same event." She smiled and patted my back. "I really want you to give **us** *a chance, Kiara."*

"No, Siddhant. You'll always be a competition to me first. Nothing else. And I'll always hate you more than I would ever like you."

She will always hate me more than she'll ever like me. *She meant her words. She always did.* She tried everything to get the number one spot, but I had a lot more expertise in my work. I remembered when Sharma uncle asked me if I could get some money when he had a crisis, I promised I'll work as much as I could to get my company where it is right now.

A billion, or more. *"Siddhant, do not forget your name, ever. Trust me, your only competition is you."* Sharma uncle told me once and I've only followed this rule, all my life. My only competition has always been me and I would always win it, *Strawberry and me were always like minds.* It was just that, her competition was another human.

"Siddhant, you wouldn't understand why I chose this company and my career over you." I had forgotten everything the day I heard those words, but I did not come back to you. For three years, until you hit your

millionth mark, I promised myself to never pester you and your journey.

And I have kept my promise, love. But now, there's nothing stopping you. You have a career, you have proven yourself to be the Businesswoman of the Year. You have achieved everything you told me you wanted, then what is stopping you to accept your feelings? What is stopping you to come back and kiss me so hard that I die?

I'd always wait for the day. For how long it takes.

Chapter 20

SIDDHANT

I entered the place, all decked up in a black suit coat. Aryan entered behind me. He had asked no question after I told him that I have decided to give Kiara some time to decide what she wants.

I knew the answer, she was going to choose her career. *Was I ready to hear it today, again?* I had no expectations anyway, ever. I moved towards the stage. We were co-hosts for the event today. My eyes searched for the one person who still hadn't arrived. Was she even coming today?

I hope she does. I hope she sees herself achieve the shares. I opened my phone to dial her when I felt her. I inhaled the rosy velvet scent that entered my nose as soon as I saw her entering.

Elegant skirt design, fishbone at the waist cut in a long style to lengthen the height. The fabric selected polyester material, soft and appealing. Sweetheart neck, silver gown with a drapey skirt tail details. The design of the gown highlighting her temperament, her goddess dressing.

My eyes softened looking at her as she looked at me. I passed her my hand as she walked towards the stage, she took it and got up. I looked at her and she raised her brows. I sighed and nodded.

"Do you plan on never talking to me, Strawberry?" She smiled and looked back. "Focus on the party and finish the guy, Goenka. I need to go home and complete my book. I chuckled, softly. One week had done something, I had no idea.

Oberoi had been meeting everyone with pride, he had me and Ahuja on board. We waited until the lights went off and the spotlight went on the TV behind Oberoi. He grinned wide. He was waiting for something else as his eyes went wide when the shares page opened and his shares started falling. Kiara looked at me and smirked. *She was really happy.*

I looked at the gate as the police entered. "What is this happening?" I heard another voice. Uh huh, the second lead in the project. Rohan Oberoi, the brat. I smirked as he came towards me. "What have you done?"

"Nothing that the world shouldn't know." I answered honestly as the police locked his father.

He glared at me before going behind the police.

"Good evening, ladies and gentlemen." Kiara wished, taking the mic. "Mr. Oberoi has been working with computer bots to raise his share prices. Goenka and I had come together to expose him when he approached us with the deal. The project you have put all your hard-earned money into will be continued, with just Ahuja

Group and Goenka Group working together. We hope you support us."

"All thanks to Ms. Ahuja," I raised my glass as everyone cheered for Kiara. Her eyes glistened and she looked at me. Her shares price went up by 80% and my shares had a spike of 20%, a half billion dollar increase, maybe. Who cared, it was her who had her biggest win today. And all I wished was that she reached more heights.

"Shall I have the honor to dance with the partner in business?" I asked as we approached the dance floor. She smiled and shook her head. "No wonder you call me your date again."

"I wouldn't." I nodded and blinked. *She didn't want it. So, I don't want it either.* We moved towards the dance floor as I pulled her closer and swayed along the music. Her scents mixed and her chest heaved. The sweetheart didn't really help me and now her body reacting to my touch. I wish she accepted it just like her body.

"You sure you don't want to fuck me in the car, love?" I whispered as I back hugged her and picked her up, twirling her. She slipped back into my arms turning back, "Not sure," I smirked as she slapped my face softly and left the dance floor.

We ended up in a corner, like our internship days. I sighed. "I am done socializing. I am NEVER HOSTING A PARTY." She whispered and I nodded.

"Kiara, I am sorry," She looked at me suddenly. "I don't know if you'd like it, but here's something." I pulled her outside, and her hands covered her mouth in shock. "No way you did that!"

“Mhm, I did.” I smiled as she ran towards a red McLaren standing outside. She looked at me, “This is for me?”

“I don’t see anyone who loves red that much.” I smiled as she jumped on me. “If that’s a way of convincing me, it is working.”

“Now I wish it was!” I shouted as she sat inside the car. I opened my phone to click a picture, her original, happiest face. Her true, feminine side. *Her real side.*

She grazed the car and came towards me. “You don’t know how much this means to me. This car is VERY EXPENSIVE.”

“Oh shit, I have a ton of money.” I chuckled and she hugged me again. “If I don’t leave right now, I am afraid I might kiss you.” She whispered and kissed my earlobe before running away. Sitting inside the car, she drove it away.

And I had nothing to do, but to go inside and suffer. *Oh Strawberry, you’ll be the death of me.*

The party was finally over and people had left. I went inside to pick up a beer before leaving when I found Aryan drinking. “What is wrong with you?”

“I am good, you fucker.”

“Okay, what happened?”

“I have a surprise for you.” I raised my brows as he said that. The lights turned off again and the screen switched to a video call. It was Mr. and Mrs. Sharma, my closer-than-parents.

“Well, Sid, you have forgotten us.” Aunty scolded me on the video call and I laughed. This boy is crazy. I looked at Uncle who just showed his thumbs up. "So proud, Siddhant. More than this romance-son of ours!" Aryan sulked as I smirked at him. I didn't care if my parents had abandoned me once, I obviously was given a set of another.

"Thank you, uncle. And Aunty, we promise we'll be home for Diwali." I promised and aunty smiled. "Beta, take care of yourself. And call us if you ever need anything. I am sure this boy doesn't help at all." Aunty lambasted her son and I laughed on his face. "Mom, I didn't call you to do my bezzati."

"Oh you did," Uncle remarked and I nodded. Aryan ran behind me as I punched him. I laughed and realized something.

Everything suddenly made sense. Everything was suddenly clear in front of me.

"Okay boys, have a fun night." The parents wished and cut the call. "I have to leave."

"Not her again,"

"It is always her." I patted his back as I ran outside. Sitting inside my car I drove to Marine Drive hoping I didn't choose the wrong place.

Chapter 21

KIARA

I sat on Marine Drive, my eyes closed. I felt peace, I felt calmness. Something I hadn't felt a whole week. He was deep into finding me, not knowing I haven't found myself yet, what would he get?

The pain. The betrayals. The life.

Every experience of my life had been so complicated that even I didn't know that being happy was my choice or being correct was it.

"And I'll always hate you more than I would ever like you." I was the one to say this statement and I never really went back on my words. I never wanted to, unlike now.

I felt like running into his arms and crying my heart out.

I felt like telling him everything I couldn't, three years ago.

I felt like I could be treated well. Or maybe, *I could be loved.*

But it wasn't nice. It wasn't something he deserved. He deserved somebody who was equally wanting to work it out. He deserved a way better human than me.

An unloved childhood. A betrayed friendship. I had got everything to change my heart into a stone. And when I had, he wanted the coal to become a diamond.

And even if they occurred in the same mine, a coal is always a coal and a diamond always remains a diamond. And I had a heart of coal.

It hurted when he slept with her on farewell. The way Gupta shouted in the whole campus about sleeping with Siddhant, it broke my heart. I wish I had said yes that day. But I couldn't.

Siddhant was my biggest competition and since the day my parents had seen him, Shanaya wanted him. My sister had a huge crush on the guy I adored. Maybe, I liked him too.

But my career was the most important thing for me. Maybe because I wanted to prove it to the world, and specifically my parents that I wasn't a loser.

I wasn't a weak child.

I was the strongest.

And what did it cost me? Siddhant's heart.

Did I care? No.

Do I care? Yes.

Does it really help? No.

My complicated brain wasn't his to solve. My problems weren't his to deal with. My heart wasn't his to save, because I broke his. As much as I hated his betrayal, there was a corner in my heart who believed this never happened.

I was pulled out of my thoughts as I heard brakes. I recognised that scent from a mile away. It was him.

How?

Here?

I looked behind as he passed a tub of ice-cream to me. I chuckled. *What in the world have I done?* Why God, why do you send him to me again and again?

"I need answers, Strawberry." He said silently. His body fixed, his body failing to gather courage. "We don't have to talk, Sid."

"I don't have to. You do." He pronounced. "There hasn't been one day I haven't thought about seeing you cry that day in square number one, saying how I wouldn't understand why you denied me that day. I want to understand. Explain to me."

"I cannot." I smiled. "Throw out words, I will make the meaning out of it." He looked at me, and I ate the ice-cream. "You sometimes make it difficult for me, Siddhant."

I closed my eyes and pulled him into a kiss. He gave in and pulled me closer. Without breaking the kiss, I was in his lap as his hand lingered all over my body. The kiss tender, the emotions dense. As much as I hated breaking him again, this was the only thing I needed.

Those rough lips, that spicy vinegar scent, that beautiful face under moonlight. There was no fight for dominance, our lips just moved together in sync until he was breathless.

I broke the kiss and looked at him, "It was your family." He whispered, panting. "I wish this was the only reason."

"Talk to me, Kiara."

"Stay nerd, you nerdy." I chuckled before pecking his lips again.

I hate to run away from difficult situations. But this guy made it impossible for me to not fuck him right there. And it was not healthy to have sex with your business rival, was it?

"Siddhant,"

He looked back, sighing. "You're an idiot." I screamed and went to my car as the sun rose.

Chapter 22

SIDDHANT

I sighed as she left. I knew a lot about her, still I knew nothing. I felt bad, of course I did, but it didn't matter more than what she was going through.

I had no idea why she didn't want to give us a chance, but if me being around gave her peace, I'd be around as nothing.

It was morning and I drove back home. The gate was locked and I saw somebody waiting outside. A five foot three girl, looking like some professional, stood outside, waiting. I went closer and she looked at me.

"Umm, good morning. I am here to meet Mr. Sharma." She informed and I nodded. I opened the door through the key I had and went inside. Aryan was dancing on the table with headphones on and I knew why she had to stand outside.

The girl started laughing seeing him while I just exhaled. It has been a regular site of visit for me for a long time. "Good morning, Mr. Sharma." I wished as he looked at me. He saw the woman beside me and jumped down the table. *Wow. That's new.*

I smirked at his reaction and he removed his headphones. "Good morning, Ms. Verma." He wished as she smiled at him. "I am sorry for disturbing you early in the morning, but the costumes were almost done and shoot started today so I had to show them to you." She described her reason for arrival.

Oh, was she the costume designer for the movie? Guess, she was. I sat on the couch as I saw them discuss. This guy didn't shift his glance away since he had seen her. *He definitely liked her.* No debate.

I was sitting casually and listening to their discussions when Aryan looked at me. I smirked and he smiled. "Ms. Verma, meet Siddhant, he's my brother."

"Oh, who doesn't know him!" She smiled and I nodded. "Good to have you on board, I like the designs you just showed." I appreciated her and Aryan smiled at me. He knows I wouldn't do it normally. I got up to freshen up when my phone rang.

Strawberry

"Is it Kiara?" Aryan asked as I picked up the phone with a smile. I rolled my eyes and picked up the phone. "Morning, Strawberry."

"Morning, I had forgotten my own car at the party place..." I cut her off as she said that. "I've sent it to your place already."

"Thank you, I'll see you in the meeting." She said and hung up the phone. *She wanted to know if I was fine.* She was just like me, her actions proved more than her words. "Mr. Goenka, how do you know Ms. Ahuja?" I heard Ms. Verma say. I looked at her and before I could answer, Aryan summarized, “Kiara is Sid’s business partner. It’s all over social media now.”

“Oh, I wanted to meet her.” She admitted her wish and smiled. “Oh she’ll love your designs,” Aryan chimed. “Why?” I felt a little inquisitive on why she wanted to meet Kiara. She looked or felt like somebody I knew.

I don’t know, but her voice was a heard one. Voices are deceitful, maybe. “I am really inspired.” She answered and I nodded. *That makes sense.* But I still didn’t believe her.

Excusing myself, I quickly went to my room and dialed Mira. “Hello, sir.” She picked up the phone in one ring. “Hey, Mira, how is the movie going on?”

“Absolutely amazing, thanks again for the chance, Sir.” She thanked me again. “Mira, you deserve the chance, anyways, I wanted to know about Ms. Verma. Is she the designer?”

“Oh yes, Adhya is the designer. She’s unquestionably the closest to the designs we required.” She acknowledged her again. Adhya Verma. This name was very familiar, why do I feel I know this name.

“Mira, can you send me her resume and portfolio?”

“Sure sir, give me time till EOD.” She affirmed. “Thank you Mira, have a great day.”

“Likewise, sir.” She wished and I hung up the phone. I went for a bath and got ready for the meetings I had today.

Will I ever be able to know the reason for her denial?

Will I ever be able to move on without knowing why we didn't get a chance?

Will she ever be able to understand that I was enough for us both until she wanted *us?*

I need to stop thinking about Kiara. I need to start going back to the promise, maybe the timeline isn't over yet. I opened my schedule for the day.

Meet the designer for my movie
PS- Sharma orders.

I shook my head, now this guy had entered my schedule. I rolled my eyes and looked forward to the day.

Meet Ms. Ahuja for the first discussion on the architecture project.

How do I even plan to avoid her? For the next six months, we were working together. I shrugged my thoughts away and went outside.

Adhya and Aryan were looking into each other's eyes, I cringed. Okay, as much as I was happy our flamboyant boy was looking into one woman's eyes, seeing him do that was puk-able. I rolled my eyes and rushed outside, without disturbing them.

Adhya Verma, who are you?

"Good morning, Mr. Goenka." Kiara's secretary wished me. I nodded as my team followed. We were meeting at the Ahuja group for our first discussion today. My team was all ready with their presentations and as much as I had heard, her team was a punctual and practical one. They made us sit in their presentation room and we waited for the boss lady to arrive.

Her team was already here and ready with their part, for the first time, they didn't know why their boss wasn't on time. *Ah, Kiara. You know how to make a man wait.*

Strawberry finally entered the presentation room, with her laptop. She nodded once at me and we settled on our chairs. Her team started first and to be honest, I was impressed. Maybe I was also impressed because I didn't really listen to anything they said, my eyes were always on the charming boss of theirs. She had realized my gaze on her a lot before, and looked away not meeting my eyes.

Maybe, it was a torture for her, but the amount of weight I had, a little torture wasn't bad. Was it? I didn't move my stare, nobody noticed. Even if they did, they did not speak. The meeting was going fine when she suddenly stood up and went outside.

Where is the Kiara Ahuja who never ran away? What was wrong with her?

I excused myself and went behind her, she stood alone in the corner of the corridor, panting. Is she anxious?

"Strawberry-"

"Goenka, leave me alone." She spat in anger, *or anxiety*. "Calm down, first. I am not going anywhere."

"LEAVE ME ALONE. You need to stay away from me. I understand this project is important for both of us but I do not want you around me."

"Says who."

"Says the girl who HATES her business rival. Says the girl who doesn't want you. Says the girl who knows you're harmful to her." She lambasted. I sighed as she held herself. "Are you sure you don't want me around you?"

"Cent percent." She affirmed strongly and I pulled myself back. I went back to the meeting. If that's what she wants, let us do it this way. Until you beg me, love, you I won't stare a glance at you.

I went back to the meeting and settled down. She came back after 15 minutes and sat down. Her team asked her if they could continue and she nodded.

No apologies, but she knows I didn't need one.

The meeting ended and our briefing with the other team started. We both exchanged sides and started discussing the points we discovered in the presentation with the other side. It was a method of mixing the groups. As much as I hated socializing, my meetings were more spoken than my usual self.

"Ms. Sumara, your point seems to be correct, but you still need to work on your design." I told Sumaira, her confidence was good, but her designs lacked. And it wasn't a good point. She came closer to me as I finished the briefing and stood on the side.

"Mr. Goenka, I heard you are perfect with your designs." I looked at her, she shifted closer. "How about we discuss it somewhere more private?" Her fingers trailed down my arm, her eyes inviting. She bit her lips, smiling. "Excuse me."

I excused myself quickly. I didn't flirt with women. And especially in an office. I got a call from Aryan and I went outside.

"Hey, I need your help." His voice was urgent. "What happened?"

"Adhya wanted to meet Kiara, can we make that happen?" I groaned. That was urgent? "I am in a meeting, we will discuss this over dinner."

"You are LOVE!" He shouted and hung up the phone. I turned back to find Sumara standing dangerously close to my face. I pulled back instantly. "I heard you don't like face contact, Mr. Goenka."

I had a certain way of declining women when they tried such attempts, but it was harsh. And I didn't know if she could stand my harshness. Before I could tell her to fuck off, another hand pulled her back from coming close to me.

Sometimes I feel I am the luckiest. Sometimes I feel, when they say *everything happens for a reason,* I love the reason it happens for.

"Sumara, do not show me your face again. Leave, you're fired." Kiara announced and Sumara shivered. She obviously didn't expect her boss to react that way. Even I didn't expect her boss to react that way. "Didn't you hear me clearly, honey?" Kiara asked again when Sumara nodded. "Collect your belongings and leave..."

"But..."

"LEAVE." Kiara parroted in a harsh tone and left. All I had to do was admire her there.

Chapter 23

KIARA

THAT *BITCH*.

I had noticed her trying to get close to Siddhant. The amount of fire that burned inside me when she got close to him was unexplainable. Sumara was one of the most confident women I had hired, but I'd hire more confident people who wouldn't go around flirting with *my* business partner.

Only mine.

I hated him, but he was mine to hate.

I disliked him, but he was mine to dislike.

I wanted to kill him, but he was only *mine* to kill.

I wanted to strangle him and kiss him and kill him and lick him, all at the same time. I hated all that I felt for him, *other than hate*. But I hated that I hated him too.

'A girl never forgets the first guy she loves', I had heard.

'But a girl also never forgets the first guy she hates.' Liz Bauxbaum had told me.

As much as I wanted to deny the fire, it burnt me more to accept it.

I looked at Siddhant as Sumara left. I pulled his hands and took him to my cabin, our conversation was too private to be done in an open corridor. He walked behind as I pulled him, conveniently, without a complaint.

I closed the gate of my cabin and pushed him towards the wall. Going close to him, I glared directly into his eyes. **"Let another woman touch you, Goenka and *I'll make sure she doesn't even find a place in hell.*"** I whispered, as his hands rapidly grabbed my body and twisted me, until I was under him. With a wall behind me, I exhaled as he grinned.

"If I let another woman touch me ever, Strawberry, *you can make sure I don't find a place in hell, either.*" He promised and grinned. Before I could push him and leave, his grip tightened around my waist and pulled me back. "On that note, are you jealous?"

"No."

"Are you not able to accept that you have the same fire burning inside you, love?"

I kiss him, biting his lips harshly. Placing my hands on his jaw, I looked deep into his blue eyes.

Ocean blue eyes, looking in mine.

I feel like I might, sink and drown and die.

"*You're a cigarette, Siddhant*. You are *dangerous* to me and yet I am *addicted* to you." I exhaled on his lips as he found my lips again. Instead of pushing him back, or pulling back, I started fighting for dominance. He picked me up as my legs wrapped around his torso and reached my table.

He sat on my chair and pulled me strongly. My body slammed on his crotch. His tongue entered my mouth as if it was his only chance, as if I'd never let him kiss me again. *Impossible.*

I hated how perfect his lips felt on mine. I hated how perfect his hands traveled on my body. I hated how senselessly he kissed me. I hated how my wildness turned into a calm silence when he dominated me.

The more I wanted to stay away from him, the more we landed up in each other's mouths, tasting tongues, and suppressing moans.

"I hate to be addicted to you,"

"Yet you are," Small whisper and his lips slid on my neck skin. And I had no answer to that question.

His hands gripped on my waist again and made me sit on the table. He slammed his palm on my thighs and parted them away. Pressing himself in, his hands made me curl my legs on his torso. While he kept licking my neck like a starving man. He kissed me again, sucking on my lower lip.

Rough. Desperate. Violent.

That is how our kiss felt.

"Siddhant," I moaned inside his mouth as he pinched my clit before his hands went inside my pants. His movements, rough and desperate. “You told me to stay away, Strawberry, and now, I cannot.” He grudged and spanked my ass, harshly. A sudden jolt of pleasure felt inside and goosebumps appeared on my body. He entered inside with his two fingers and I jumped. He slammed them in again, unforgiving.

“Ah, Siddhant!” I screamed as he pinched my clit again. He increased the pace of his fingers and my body moved along in the movement. He suppressed my moans by kissing me again, but yet they were audible. *Inaudible, outside- thankfully.*

Few more movements.

Few more strokes.

Few more kisses.

I exploded.

I exploded with a hard orgasm.

I gasped and broke the kiss as he pulled the fingers out and shoved them inside my mouth. “Taste yourself, Strawberry.”

The salty taste of my body fluids entered my mouth and before I could lick it off, he pulled back and tasted it himself. All I could see was him, licking my juices off like it was ice-cream.

I was unable to guess what were his next moves as he quickly readjusted my pants and pulled me down from the table. “We’re done with our break, darling. Let’s go and do some work.”

Uh huh, I would never be able to work on my table the same way again.

And there was nothing in the world that could hold me back from giving in to what he asks.

We worked further for the entire day after that and he made sure I didn't get up from my seat. As rough he was on my table three hours ago, as nice he was throughout the whole meeting. There was a smirk plastered on his face after that. And there was nothing which could stop it.

Of course.

We finished the meeting and everyone left for their squares and blocks leaving me and Siddhant alone.

"Kiara," He came towards me, my heart thudded again. "I want you to go on a date with me," He proposed.

I can't.

I can't.

He's my business rival.

"I will go with you." *GODDAMN YOU HEART.*

He smiled and kissed my cheek softly. "Since I'd been really rough today, love." He winked and left.

I blushed.

I blushed.

I am smitten.

I think I am getting obsessed.

Chapter 24

SIDDHANT

I entered my house with Aryan standing near the dining table again. I groaned. I had lost all control with Kiara today, and all I needed was a release.

"I'll be in my room for some time." I said without listening to him and went to my room. I needed a long bath. I stripped and entered the shower.

.

Freshened up, I went outside. Aryan gave me a what-is-wrong-with-you look while I shrugged. I sat on the dining table as he came and stood beside my chair again. "Hey, don't tell me you tried cooking again."

"Well no, Adhya did." He told and sat down, opening two bowls of my favorite *chole chawal* and I looked at him wide-eyed. "You guys cooked together?"

"Mhm," He blushed as I was clearly teasing him. "She wants to meet Kiara, can we?"

"Oh, on that, wait a moment." I opened my phone and saw what Mira had sent me. I opened Adhya Verma's resume and my eyes went wide on the first information it gave. Adhya belonged to the Nationals.

I looked up from my phone and Aryan looked at me questioningly. "Call Adhya."

"Right now? It's late..." He asked again and I got up from my seat. "We're going to meet her."

"Will you tell me what happened?" He asked while I rushed outside picking up my car keys. "She is from Nationals."

"So?"

"That's the same college Kiara went to." I claimed and he looked at me, confused. Of course, it was confusing. If Kiara and Adhya went to the same college then why does she want to meet her through us? And was it her voice that I heard three years ago?

Square SEVEN. Adhya Verma. She was present on the first day of the internship. She knew Kiara.

"Wait! I know what it is. Kiara is the best friend Adhya mentioned that day."

"Which day?"

"On the day I found her in the club, drunk and crying." He explained. *Hein?*

This guy was confusing me.

We reached her place and he rang the bell. Adhya opened the door and her eyes went wide seeing us. "Aryan," *First names*. Sure there is a thing. "You went to Nationals, you know Kiara..." Aryan spat out words and she looked at me.

"You- you know-" She pointed at me, falling backwards. Aryan quickly caught her before she could fall as she started crying. "Siddhant- I am sorry-" She hiccuped and cried. "Adhya, I am not here to blame you. Just tell me what happened."

She looked at me, hopeful. "Kiara hates me." She started the story as we waited and sat down.

ADHYA

I looked at Siddhant and Aryan as they waited for me to continue with the story. I didn't know what they would choose to do in the end. I knew I was one to be blamed, I knew I was the one at fault.

But everyone deserves a chance, don't they?

"Kiara and I had been friends since the start of college. I had always been interested in fashion designing and Kiara used to model for me, in the start of my portfolio. She was my best friend, until one day I ruined everything."

Siddhant sighed and waited for me to continue. This guy was smitten by my best friend since the first day. The only day I came to the internship, to deny working in it.

"Kiara!!!!" I shouted from my square as she got up and turned back at me. Siddhant was one of the most handsome men I had seen and I already knew my best friend had a chance with him. She came towards me and raised her brows asking. "I got an internship at the fashion house!"

"Oh my god! I am so happy for you!" She jumped in happiness. I didn't join her in the internship after that, but she kept telling me about Siddhant sometimes.

I always knew every insecurity she had, everything from her parents, to her academic low scoring. To her unbelieving mind and her sweetest heart, I adored everything about her.

She was my best friend.

"I was the one you heard, Siddhant." He nodded. "I knew it, I already guessed it."

"She doesn't hate you. But what I have done has broken her heart. And she is not ready to give it to somebody whom she broke." I told Siddhant as he sighed. I knew what he felt, but I didn't have a reply on how I could help.

"What happened between you two?" Aryan asked and I smiled sadly. "I had a fashion show to style and it was a competition. I asked her to model and she agreed. But when the event started, I saw her walk for my rival. And I couldn't take that, maybe because it was my first event as a stylist and I couldn't even take part, and also because my rival won it because of her. Her confidence, her style, her sense of fashion was always unmatched."

"Listen to me, listen Adu-" I didn't let Kiara speak. I raised my hand as she tried coming close. Tears ran down her eyes, but I didn't budge. She had betrayed me, modeling for somebody else was the last thing she should have done. She knew how badly I needed it. She knew how desirable I was.

I didn't ask what made her do it. I didn't want to know why she did it. She did it, which was the end for me.

"Why Kiara? I was always the first one to cheer for you when you got something, then how did you do this to me? How do you even have the courage to stand here and try to talk to me? Did you try to think once before doing this?"

Kiara shuddered as I screamed on her face. She didn't utter a word and let me scream. I felt hurt, maybe I didn't realize this could have been the biggest mistake I was making.

"You feel like the biggest mistake I ever made." I shouted. "Please, listen to me once." She tried to pacify me, but I didn't listen.

"Kiara, do not show me your face, ever again." I whispered and left the place. I did not turn back ever again.

"It wasn't her mistake. She was blackmailed to do it. My rival was one of the richest girls in the college and she threatened her that she'll end my career if Kiara didn't walk for her. Kiara sacrificed everything to save my career and what did I do? I didn't even give her a chance to explain." I couldn't stop as tears ran down my eyes.

Aryan was quick enough to pull me into his arms.

Aryan Sharma.

Brown hair. Hazel eyes. Handsome face.

The most unexpected entry in my life, yet the most beautiful one. We started off as friends on the movie set but we both knew there was something more to it.

Aryan and I had met on the set of soulmates but I knew him since before. And I had a huge crush on him. If Kiara would have been here, she would have always tried putting us together. And I couldn't help, he has always been too sweet to me.

"So, how did you get to know?" I chuckled hearing that question. "Last year, at the Fashion Week. I couldn't believe my eyes when I saw my rival working under one of my friend's stylists. When I met her, she told me how even blackmailing Kiara couldn't help her in her career. I swear, I died at that point." I briefed them and Siddhant and Aryan looked at each other.

"Look, Siddhant, I really need to meet her once. I have tried the application to style her, but she knows it is my firm. She will never accept it." I pleaded and Aryan rubbed my back. "Only if you accept Aryan is a pain in ass." Siddhant's mouth curved into something, a small smile if I guessed correctly.

Aryan chuckled and I grinned. "Thank you Adhya, you solved the leftover puzzle for me." Siddhant thanked me and I shook my head. "If you hurt her, I will murder you." I threatened and he nodded. "I will make sure,"

"I'll leave you two now, enjoy the time." He added and moved out of the house in a swift movement. Kiara was always right, ***he had a face colder than ice and heart warmer than fire.*** And the heart always thudded for her.

Now I was sure he would keep her safe. ***Even from herself.***

Chapter 25

SIDDHANT

I knew everything now. Every insecurity, every disbelief, every indecisive decision in her head.

Kiara's heart was twisted so much that she had stopped accepting what it said.

I knew why she didn't give *us* a chance.

I knew why she didn't *accept* her feelings.

I knew why she *hated* me.

Because she couldn't trust me enough, she couldn't trust herself enough. As I promised myself, I didn't come in between her dreams, unrealizing that her dream was not her career. It was how to make her heart a stone.

She succeeded in the majority of it, but I had my ways. I chuckled to myself.

I was going on a date with Kiara Ahuja. *My Strawberry*. An official date and I already felt giddy.

Will she love what I had planned?

Will she like me back?

Will she accept me?

As much as I wanted her to, it will always be her *decision*. Something, she was never given a chance to take.

I will let her live.

I will take all the responsibilities she was forced to take.

I will make sure she is ***happy***.

I planned the date, making sure everything was perfect. Aryan had helped me with some things which were more understood to him about her likes. He explained to me a lot about her book love and I already knew what would make her happy.

Adhya told me how she missed her childhood. She missed those childish moments, she loved reading. She was fond of fashion. She loved the pasta I made for her.

I mentally noted everything. It was my only chance, who knows the last one. Everything had to be perfect, just like how she liked it.

Some old places, some new places, some perfect places. Everything about the day was set.

Strawberry- How should I dress tomorrow? I mean, casual or fancy?

I smiled seeing her message. She was excited about the date, and it made me feel *ecstatic*.

Me- Dress casual, I'll pick you up at 10 am tomorrow.

Strawberry- 10 am? I thought the date was just a dinner.

Me- Well, wrong thoughts. Be ready by 10.

Strawberry- Are you ordering me, Goenka?

Me- Not at all, love. Please be ready by 10.

I shook my head, she was too stubborn to accept things. Let's go to sleep early today. I made sure everything was done for tomorrow and arrived back home.

"Are you serious?" I heard Aryan shout. He was on the phone, it was Adhya most probably. Our little-lover boy was whipped for her. *Like I wasn't.*

Wow, are my thoughts also mocking me now? I quickly finished my dinner and went to my room. If I think I am planning to sleep early, I don't see that happening. I was too nervous.

GO TO SLEEP SID.

Chapter 26

KIARA

10 AM.

What was he planning to do? Take me out for breakfast? I chuckled at my thoughts.

I was going out with SIDDHANT. I was going on a date with my business rival. I still can't believe I said yes. But how did it affect me? I was up at 7 am in the morning to look the prettiest.

I didn't plan to do a lot of effort, but was it going according to the plan? HAHA YOU WISH. I took a long shower, washing my hair. I am not sure what was going to happen today, 10 am and the whole day. This guy was already making me nervous.

I wore a simple outfit, a red flowing knee length floral dress, with a cinched waist and a v-neck. I was not sure of how much I had to walk but I still picked up my red heels to match with my dress. I picked up my phone, I wasn't planning to carry any purse. Soft loose curls, which suited the best to my chocolate hair, and a soft nude shade on the lips. I was all ready to see him.

I heard the doorbell ring and I bolted downstairs. Lata Didi had opened the gate to Siddhant and he stood there in a red gray combination tee and pants, he knew I'd wear red. He smiled at me as he strolled towards him. I looked at Lata Didi once before leaving. She smiled, as if she knew.

He opened the gate of the car, without speaking a word. I sat inside and he followed. "Good morning, Kiara. You look ravishing." *The way he said my name already made my stomach clench.* I smiled at his compliment, "Thank you, Sid. You look good too, now will you tell me where we are going?"

"Patience, Strawberry." He started driving as we reached the first place we met, our internship company's office branch in Mumbai. "Let's start from the first place." He opened the gate and passed his hands. I smiled before giving my hand to him. He pulled me and kept his hands on my waist as we paced inside. He took me directly to the canteen, but it was not open. I couldn't see one staff member there.

"Is the office shut?" I asked, my voice lighter. "Yeah, I asked them to shut it for one day, small money and everyone agrees." *The money was not small. I am sure.* But these Billionaire guys!

"Good morning ma'am, here's your breakfast." I shook my head seeing the person who served, *Aryan Sharma*, the best friend, the best selling author, working as a waiter. I chuckled seeing the breakfast, a *vadapao*, and a small cup of *chai*. Like the good old days, like the internship days.

We both had our breakfasts, laughing at the crazy things we did in our internship. No pressure, no outside world problems, no tension, everything was just beautiful. I wish we could ever go back and live that time again. I finished my breakfast and looked at him, struggling to eat the last piece. "You still can't finish it?"

"I haven't had one in the last three years!" He mumbled, his voice hoarse. That was said normally, but it felt deep inside me. *I haven't had one in the last three years,* I believe you. "You're cheesier than you say."

"I am a businessman, come on." He cleaned his face with a tissue and rolled his eyes. He got up and smirked at me, "Ready for the next thing, love?"

"Very much." I answered, something about this day was different. I felt leaving all the worries behind, I felt like being myself, I felt like living it. And before my overthinking brain could shut this feeling down, my heart had already given into it. I was all set to enjoy the day, I would live it whole. Siddhant made me sit inside the car and drove towards the first architectural building we designed together.

We were the best project team in our internship. He stopped the car under it and looked at me. "Feeling nostalgic?"

"Too much!" I looked at it and grinned proudly. It was my first design, not that perfect but beautiful if I see it today. "Do you wanna go inside?" He asked, his eyes shining. "Sure!" I answered quickly. We both went inside and saw the changes made into it, it looked like Goenka's work. "Did you pick this up again?"

"Quite a year ago, sweetheart." He smiled, brushing his lips over my head. I glanced at the design and sighed. "What's next?"

"I am hoping you'll love that the most." He avowed and I shuffled my expressions, trying to guess what it could be. He passed me a chit before turning into the alley which I loved the most. The car stopped near *THE BOOK NOOK,* my favorite bookstore in the city. I watched him open the gate for me and I came out, he didn't let me open the chit yet. We went inside and I grinned.

The best place to take me out on a date, *and he knew it.* I glanced at him once, before he pointed at the chit. I opened it and it said,

Love is ordinary mundane, and Stella, you're extraordinary.

I quickly ran towards the romance section and shuffled through the books to find the book this quote was written from. One of my favorite books in the series, I opened it to find another chit.

If it was a game, *I love the idea,* Sid. You have already won me. I opened the next chit and it said, ***No, it's not a treasure hunt. The question is, you mentioned three book names in our internship days and I still remember the names. Do you?***

I remember every single moment I have spent with you, Siddhant. As much as I hated to remember it, I loved every bit of it. I quickly rushed to find the first book I mentioned to him.

First.

Second.

Third.

I got the three chits from each of the books I had mentioned to him and opened them to find another line.

"Maybe I am your business rival, but if you wanted, my business and I would be on our knees for you." I started crying. This guy remembered everything, this man *remembered* every single detail. I turned back to find him standing there. "I am going to make sure you have an endless TBR and a library to sit and read, and I am also going to make sure *to do whatever you read to you whenever you feel like.*"

I gulped, his blue eyes winking at me as he finished. I didn't care who was around as I decreased the distance between us and kissed him. He smiled shamelessly, lingering his hands on my waist, and kissing me deeper. Everything around me was blurr, all I had was Siddhant on my head. All I needed, was ***him***. And I had never questioned my choices before.

"We have a lot for you to do, Kiara." He whispered, I exhaled in his mouth. "And what is that?"

"Come, let me show you," His eyes stared at my body for a few moments, but then he quickly realized and smiled. Pointing a finger at the box on the table, he showed 2 chits to me. "Choose one,"

"What is in it?" I asked, curiously. I never felt more fun, I have never spent more time on gifts. I have never been given so many surprises. "One has got 2 boxes written on it, within 15 minutes. You can pick up as many books as you like in those two books."

"And the other one?" I was quick enough to shout with all enthusiasm. He grinned, "The other one has three boxes but 10 minutes." I smiled, I don't need more time. I chose one of the chits and he passed me.

THREE BOXES IN 10 MINUTES.

"Alright, watch me," I winked and ran inside with all the three boxes. Straight into the romance section, I picked up all the books I could see. I kept filling the three boxes behind me, trying to ignore Siddhant leaning on the bookshelf and looking at me as if he would eat me.

I definitely want him to eat me. You're crazy Kiara, BOOKS.

"Times up." He jabbered as he stopped me. I squinted my eyes at him as he smiled and pecked my lips.

"You can read all of them first, then I'll bring you here again." He affirmed and I beamed. We both reached outside and he passed his card to pay for the books. *It just looked like the Amex cards from the books.* I chuckled to myself and he looked at me, raising a brow. I shook my head and we reached outside.

He started driving again and I realized I had spent a lot of time at the bookstore. The morning idea was pretty well planned. He knew I'm going to take hours. He stopped the car outside his place, and my eyes shined looking at it. His house was gorgeous, the last time I had come here, I had spent more time gawking at him cooking than looking around. This time I was going to do it, I guess.

His lips turned into a smile again as he took me inside. The house was simple, but beautiful. Aryan had kept a lot of stuff which I am sure wasn't Siddhant's type. A lip shaped table, that is what suited the sofas kept. "You want to look around?" He bowed his head towards me and I nodded.

He took me to the study room and I gasped. "That's Aryan's library." He informed and I looked at in awe. I had never seen a study room like that, aesthetic and architecture on its peak. I looked at him once before rushing to the books kept there. He quietly waited until I finished. "Guess what the plan is?"

"I cannot, just tell me." He smirked and moved closer to me, his body pressed up against mine, and he wrapped both his arms around me. "You're very impatient, Strawberry," He said, his voice low sending shivers down my spine. He pulled out a book from the shelf behind me and wrapped his other arm around my waist pulling me. He sat down on the chair and made me sit on his lap.

"You remember how you always complained I never spoke much, Strawberry?" I nodded at his question, my body feeling chills sitting on his lap as his hands traveled down my thighs. "Here's my life, it has everything, and all of it belongs to you."

I bent myself and turned my face softly to look at him, blinking. "Sid, I need you." I whispered, he smirked widely before sliding his hands under the hem of my dress, his hands moving up my thighs. "Are you sure about that, love?" He said, a look of desire in his eyes as his eyes met mine.

He grins, his smirk widening, "As you wish, Strawberry," He said, before grabbing my thighs again and lifting me up to turn me towards him, placing my hips on his crotch. "Sidd-" I said and his lips were on me. I closed my eyes and let him deepen the kiss. A warm kiss, his lips rougher but sweeter than ever. His hands on my waist, firm. I gripped on his hair and my tongue licked him more and more.

We were just perfect together. ***We are just perfect together.***

My lips slid on his neck and bit him while he let me. I sucked on his neck, probably giving him a hickey. My hands pressing his shoulders, or exploring his body. I already knew he had abs, but sliding fingers on his abs felt hotter than I imagined. I looked at him again, kissing him strongly, this time he let me. I sucked on his lips, biting them. I pressed his chest but his hands on my waist firmer than ever. His lips all wet from my saliva, I breathed heavier.

"Doing what I always wanted to do to you, Siddhant." I kissed his neck as his hands slid into my dress sleeves and pulled them downward. He looked at my breast for a moment and placed his mouth on them. He bit softly on my nipple and I moaned. I slowly rubbed myself on his hardened cock. His hand gently helped my hips move in rhythm, while his other hand rolled another nipple between his fingers. He sucked on my nipples, gently slowly.

My body moved sensually, sinking into him deeper and deeper. I whispered tiny moans, "I'm gonna come..." I started moving faster, forward and backward, round and round. He sucked on my nipples, stronger. Few more *strokes*, few more *bites*, few more *movements*, few more *moans*.

"Fuck," I came with a loud moan, my body pushing hard on him. I clenched on his shirt, squeezing it strongly. I still sat on his lap, my hands around his neck, my face buried into his neck. He looked at me, his blue orbs staring directly into mine, his gaze a mix of lust and adoration. His smirk, now a gentle smile, "Now let me do what I always wanted to do to you, Kiara." He picked me up, placing his rough wet lips on me.

Chapter 27

KIARA

L*ips crashing. Tongue gliding. Slight moans.*

We moved across the hall as he reached the kitchen, our kiss never stopping. My hands pressed his shoulders trying to explore his body but his movements fast enough to not let me.

Every touch, every kiss, every moan that reverberated my throat as his mouth moved on my body was like a heated pain, but pleasurable. It felt like I was swallowed by a vortex of pleasure and it is beyond describable.

His hands slowly moved down my dress as he leaned in, "I want you to tremble under my touch, Strawberry," He placed a kiss on my neck, and I gasped as he softly grazed his hands on my exposed thighs, widening them. He trailed his hands up slowly towards my heat, and my face flushed with the spark of it.

I placed my hands on his chest, as his blue orbs looked into mine when he grazed over my clothed clit delicately. I trembled under his touch, *like he wanted.* "Siddhant..." I whispered out of breath. He seemed to enjoy my moans as he looked at me admiringly, while I was already dripping under his touch. I bit my lip, as his fingers entered me. "Please..." I whimpered trying to control my moans which he *wanted* to hear as he continued in the rhythmic movement like he always did.

He always did. *He was the only one.*

"Eyes on me, Kiara." He whispered since I had closed my eyes to bite back a moan. His grip on my neck tightened forcing them to open in a moment. His whiskey voice made my heart stop as my core became wetter. He plunged his fingers deeper into my core, causing me to gasp. **"Eyes on me when I devour you, love."** He ordered and lowered himself to his knee, blowing softly on my clit.

Before I knew it, his tongue licked my thighs and latched onto me. "Fuck! You're so sweet, Strawberry," I gazed at him, my chest heaving up and down. Siddhant Goenka was on his knees for me, *out of all the people in the world,* ***it was my business rival***.

My legs shook as my body quivered in pleasure. "You're addicting," He muttered, his alluring blue eyes looking at me. His tongue worked like magic, as my head fell back due to pleasure.

"***Come inside my mouth, darling.***" He demanded as my body shuddered. I nearly lost my balance as I came. He sucked my clit, like he would never get enough of it. My heart raced, my body withering against the kitchen slab. He stood up and I could see his mouth still covered with my fluids. He placed his lips on me, making me taste myself.

"How rude of me to eat the dessert before dinner," He winked as he moved towards the shelf and took out a pan, not before making me sit. "Since you liked what I cooked, today's dinner is by me." He said, picking up the box behind me, and kissing me again.

I gawked at him while he cooked shirtless, with an apron. Every stir, every saute, every click of his fingers, everything aroused inside me.

Fuck you, romance books.

Everything about him was sexy. Every movement of this man was hot.

He realized my gaze at him and brought the noodles he made me. "Here's your food," I picked up a spoonful and ate it. He smiled as I moaned in delight. It was delicious. I put my hand in front of him as he slowly ate the noodles. Every move, seducing me.

"Next place to this house would be, the man in the house's room." He took me to his room where I looked around in awe. The room was screaming architecture, and before I could say a word about it, his lips were on me.

I felt every nerve of my body accelerate as his hands pinched my waist making me gasp. His tongue inside my mouth, he dominated the kiss, and the only thing I felt was a need between my thighs. He made me part my legs with his hands under my thighs, he pulled me closer and I felt his length against my core. I could barely hold myself together as my panties dampened again.

Realizing, he laid me against the bed and I gasped when he pulled down my underwear in one quick motion. Forcing my legs apart, he stared at me slowly pulling his pants off. I moaned softly as his hands grazed my clit again. "Can't wait to taste you again, Strawberry," He muttered and placed his mouth on my clit. My head fell back against the bed and my mouth opened. I ran my hands through his hair, his hands slowly reached my thighs again, pushing me open wider. "Ah!" I whimpered as he placed a few kisses on my core, pushing his fingers inside loosening me.

It didn't take a lot of time for his fingers to hit the right spot as my release came in full force and my leg shook in his hold. I was breathless as he pulled away and slowly ran his thumb on my clit. He unzipped my floral dress and pushed it away. His hands unhooked my bra before tossing it to the ground. Sensuously spitting on his hands, he coated his length and rubbed the tip on my core.

"I'll be gentle, but tell me if you feel any discomfort, Kiara." He leaned and whispered against my lips. He slowly pushed himself in and I felt my breath stop. I bit my lip as the pain felt unbearable. I had read every feeling that described this, but when I felt it was euphoria.

I felt on fire when he was fully inside me, he leaned in and kept kissing my neck and face softly. The way he caressed my body, the way he was *tender*, the way he did everything, I felt more aroused.

I let out a pleased hum, "Faster, Sid."

"You want faster, huh?" He muttered and I threw my head backwards as he pulled out and slammed himself into me. He went deeper and deeper, and leaned up slightly. My hips met his thrusts, "You look so pretty *getting fucked*." He drawled and my clit clenched. Every sound his mouth made, my body aroused every single bit of it. I gripped on his arms for support as his movements turned faster, my body feeling ecstasy.

Few more thrusts.

Few more strokes.

Few more moans.

I exploded. I exploded with a passionate groan. My body felt loose, "That's it, sweetheart, come with me." He spoke, his voice smoother than ever. We came together, in an almost romantic sort of way. I could feel his cum seeping deep into me, and it felt absolutely enraptured.

"Siddhant," I whispered, as he looked at me. "Let me have you a little longer,"

And I wished this never stopped. I slowly felt drowsy as he kissed my lips, covering us.

Chapter 28

SIDDHANT

I groaned as the sunshine hit my face. I looked at Kiara sleeping peacefully beside me. Every incident from the previous night flashed in front of me, and I felt ecstatic. I quickly got up and freshened up a bit, and prepared a hot water tub for her. She was sore, I was sure.

I came and sat on the bed beside her, as she moved and wrapped her arms around mine. Before I could move, her eyes opened softly. She gazed at me with admiration, and *it felt like a win.*

"Morning, Strawberry," I wished, picking up a sweatshirt from the cupboard. "I'll help you wear this, then you can take a bath." I softly placed the sweatshirt near her head and she smiled.

"You don't have to do that..."

"I am afraid you heard it like a question, love." I smirked as she blushed. *Did Kiara Ahuja just blush?* I made her wear the sweatshirt which ended on her lower thighs. She looked cute. She looked *mine.*

I could see the marks I had given her, as she got up. Her legs gave up before she could realize and I held her quickly. "Let me," I affirmed and picked her up till the washroom. "What do you want for breakfast?"

"A little more sleep," She chuckled and I smiled. *This was the real Kiara, the beautiful smile.* She closed the gate as I went outside and I heard the shower. I went outside to make her some breakfast before she could rest again. Picking up oats, I started cooking. My phone rang and I picked it up, it was a call from my company.

"Morning,"

"Good morning sir, can you let me know if you have the file of the Mathur enterprises at your place, since I can't find it in your office," My assistant asked me and I hummed. I might have kept it in the study.

"Yeah, it's here."

"Sir, can you give me the details?" I sighed, work was work. I hummed again and opened the file.

Before I could finish the sentence, I heard a shout. "I'll get back..." I hung up the phone instantly realizing it was Kiara. I rushed outside to find Kiara standing in front of Aryan and Adhya and I knew this was going to be explosive.

"What-" Before I could mutter, Kiara glared at me. "Not a word, Adhya. You know nothing about my life, and this is not the place." She shut her up. Kiara quickly marched towards my room and I followed her. "Kiara-"

"Did you know Adhya was here?" She asked me and I sighed. Her face faded and she frowned at me. "I cannot believe you knew and still let her..."

"I did not know she was going to be here today." I justified but it didn't work as Kiara picked up her phone and dress. She had taken my shorts and another sweatshirt. "Kiara,"

"You don't know the matter, Sid." She hurriedly picked up her heels. "I know more than what you think I do," I avowed and she stopped. "Adhya wants to apologize."

"For what? For making me believe in no friendships again? For making me indecisive about my entire life? Or for making me never believe in relationships? What will she apologize for?" Kiara screamed, I didn't have any answer.

"It was years ago. Forgive her, you'll feel better."

"I do not move on," She declared and I came in front of her before she could leave. "Then how did we end up here, Kiara?"

She heard my question and her patience bursted. Each tear falling down her eyes felt like unspoken words, unspoken wrath, and an unspoken feeling inside her. She fell down on her knees and started crying hysterically.

"Strawberry," I pulled her into my embrace as she hiccuped. "Cry as much as you want, I am right here." I consoled her and she nodded. "Trust me, Kiara. You'll feel better, move on." Kiara nodded softly.

She got up and I wiped her tears away. "Let anyone make you cry again, Strawberry and I will make sure that person cries all their life."

Kiara chuckled and pulled me closer, "I genuinely don't know why my brain goes blank when I look at you. I think I'm going a ***little crazy*** about you, Sid."

"That is a conversation for later, let me call Adhya." She nodded and I went outside, making her sit on the bed before leaving. Adhya looked at me and I nodded. She quickly went inside, while Aryan patted my back.

KIARA

I was in love with Siddhant Goenka.

Since always.

Since forever.

Everything that guy had ever done for me, was more than I ever expected for myself. I hadn't expected to be loved so much. I hadn't imagined being adored so much.

Adhya came inside and paused before coming closer. I gazed at her and the bed, and she understood the following. She exhaled, before she started, "Kiara, I know-"

"What do you know?" I asked calmly. Siddhant was right, I had to move on, I had to forget it. I had to forgive Adhya. "I know what I did was unforgivable, and I know it is the biggest mistake I ever made, but please Ki... just one last chance?"

"And why would I give you that chance?"

"Because you're and you'll always be the best friend I'd ever wanted." She whimpered silently. I looked at her, sitting on the verge of crying.

She was, is, will always be the best friend I ever had.

"Okay, Adhya," I affirmed and she looked at me. "I am even ready to grovel," She puppy-eyed and I chuckled. I laughed whole-heartedly. She joined me and we ended up laughing hysterically.

Like always.

"Ki, please? I swear I am never-"

"DV, we always made mistakes earlier. It was just that you and I cleared them out." I told her and she nodded. Before I could say anything else, she pulled me into a hug. "Kiaaaaarraaaa!" She screamed and I rolled my eyes.

Still the same affectionate sticky ass. "Don't call me that in your head," She complained and I smiled. We still knew what the other one thought. "I am sorry, Ki. I am really really sorry."

"Mhm, you're okay." I nodded and we didn't break the hug. The warmth this hug had, no other ever did. She was the closest to what I called a family. She didn't make me feel unwanted, or an outsider ever. Yes we made our share of mistakes, but it is over now.

My life was a little back on track, it wasn't as fucked up as it was.

"Siddhant, well, what about him?" She asked me and I smiled. I had no answer to that question yet.

I had to tell Siddhant first.

I had to talk to him first.

Crap, Adhya was my only ear. Adhya knew everything about me, and there was nothing I could ever hide from her.

“We had our first date.” I told her and she smirked. “Did you wash your hair before the date?”

“Um hmm.” She clapped and stood up excitedly. “Don’t Monica-Rachel me.”

“Oh really, sure. Lie from yourself, but not from me.” She teased and I groaned. “Hey, I just forgave you.”

“Shut up, but whatever. Come I have to give you some news.” She pulled me outside the room and Aryan and Siddhant got up seeing us. She winked at me as we walked towards them and I sighed.

You signed up for the drama again, Strawberry. Wonderful, now I’ll mock myself in a Siddhant Goenka style. We moved towards them as Adhya joined Aryan to hold his biceps, and smiled at me.

“NO WAY YOU GUYS ARE DATING.” I shouted and Adhya smiled again. Aryan looked at her in shock. Siddhant looked at them in shock. I looked at Siddhant in shock. “What do you mean you didn’t know?”

“You- you didn’t tell me that it got serious...” Siddhant’s voice broke in the middle of the sentence, as if he was betrayed. Adhya chuckled seeing that and Siddhant’s face quickly turned back. “Adhya-”

“Kiara is my best friend...” She blinked at him and he sighed. Right, Aryan was *whipped* for Adhya. He was always an Adhya coded guy. Adhya wasn’t a book reader, but I always told her she’ll fall for a reader. And guess what, I was always right.

“Siddhant-”

"Shut up." Siddhant shook his head at Aryan. Adhya and I controlled our laugh. Okay, Siddhant you're not betrayed. "Bhai-"

"No." Siddhant grunted again. "You'll be the reason for my death, Adhya." Aryan smiled helplessly at Adhya who looked at him with a lopsided smile. "Siddhant, it's okay."

"Right, it's okay." He grunted looking at Aryan again. Aryan smacked his forehead and smiled at Siddhant. "Baby-"

"Hey-" Siddhant disgressed. I looked at them and started laughing. "Siddhant, forgive him." I smiled and he nodded. "Yeah, happy for you guys." He nodded nonchalantly and I looked at Aryan, poor him. "Grovel, author sahab."

"This couple is called a groveling couple." Adhya declared and Aryan laughed. "Let's have breakfast," Siddhant sighed and everyone followed him. "Where's my phone?"

"On the desk near the couch." Siddhant informed me and Aryan got up. "I'll get it,"

"What's wrong with him?" I asked Adhya who chuckled softly. "I told him, he has to impress you if he wants to date me."

"Fuck you Verma!" I hi-fived with her as we laughed. I realized Siddhant stared at me from the kitchen and I looked at my plate quickly, my eyes never meeting his. Aryan passed me my phone before sitting beside Adhya and Siddhant served everyone breakfast.

"Siddhant, how come you never taught Aryan cooking?"

"Oh no, thank you." He joined his hands, shaking his head vigorously. I looked at him wide-eyed before I saw Adhya joining him too. "He sucks."

"I agree," Adhya chimed and Aryan looked at them in deceit. "Adu-"

"Uhm, uhm," I fake coughed and Aryan smiled. *Right he is scared.* I opened my phone and saw 100 missed calls. Who died?

Missed call- Dad- 45

Missed call- Shanaya- 56

What happened? My face paled everytime my family was concerned. "What's wrong?" Siddhant was the first one to notice and I smiled. "There is something wrong, I guess"

I dialed Shanaya and she picked up the phone in two rings. "Shanaya-"

"Where the fuck are you, Kiara?" She screamed from the other side. I pulled my phone away, and everyone stopped eating. "What is wrong-"

"Mom got ill last night and we had to take her to the hospital." She told me and I sighed. "Is she fine now?"

"We don't know the doctor is treating her. We had to shift her to Mumbai overnight." I looked at Siddhant who raised his brows, concerned. "Which hospital?"

"Gentle Hands." I sighed. Of course my family would go to the most luxurious hospital in the city, even if they were doctors themselves. We had our own branch here, what the hell are they thinking? She hung up the phone even before I could answer and everyone looked at me apprehensive. "Umm, mom got ill."

“In Mumbai?” Adhya was quicker than anyone else to ask. I hummed. “They shifted her overnight,”

“How?” Siddhant asked and I shrugged, I didn’t know myself. “I have to go and see to this,”

“We’re going with you.” They chorused and I shook my head. “Guys-”

“We’re going,” They parroted again. I sighed as Siddhant pulled me into a hug. “It’ll be fine, let’s go.” Aryan passed the keys of the Ford, Siddhant had and we all sat inside. He started driving and I looked at my watch, *I hope mom was fine.*

I was concerned. It didn’t help, she was my mother. Even if she hated me, she was my *biological* mother. I felt a hand on my thighs as he nodded. I pressed his hands to assure I was fine. *No I wasn’t.*

We reached inside and I looked for the reception. “Mrs. Ahuja.” I asked the woman at the reception. “Fourth floor, ma’am.”

I nodded and quickly ran towards the stairs. There was no time to wait for the lift.

Chapter 29

KIARA

"Go and get the reports checked," I heard Siddhant say to Aryan while he followed me. I ran up the stairs when my legs started hurting and he held me. "You're not okay."

"I can't," I pressed my legs as he picked me up quickly. "Siddhant-"

"Shut up, sweetie." He kissed my cheek before rapidly walking up the stairs. We reached the fourth floor and he made me stand softly. My heart was already melted. "Go, now."

"Come with me," I placed my hand in his and he peered at me. "You sure? They don't like me." He asked and I chuckled. "They love you and your money, just for their favorite daughter."

"Oh my god." He wheezed and I laughed again. I found Shanaya sitting on the chair and dad talking to the doctor. I went near Shanaya who got up seeing me.

"God, look who's here, the only mistake my parents made."

"Shanaya-" I intervened but she didn't stop, *you're angry because you had to manage all the stuff.* I rolled my eyes and she glared at me. "Don't roll your eyes at me again. Do you even realize how late are you? We've been trying to reach you since yesterday."

"I was busy."

"You've always been busy, have you ever had time for your family? And by the way, now that you're here, please go and pay for the commercial flight we had to take to bring mom here."

I chuckled, *here's the reason they needed me.* "Excuse me," I kept laughing until dad came near us. "Family? This is what you call a family? Who doesn't even know how their daughter is, is she alive or dead? Is she fine or not? What did she want to do in her life? What responsibilities did she want and what not? Shanaya, they're YOUR parents, and the only mistake they made was to become parents." I lashed out as she looked at me in shock. "And excuse me again, thank you for reminding me of my job, just to pay for your useless little shits."

"You chose to be an outsider, Kiara." Dad intervened and I looked at him. Uh, right. "You are the one who decided to do it against the family. You are the one who chose to go away. You're the one who picked up business when you *had* cleared your NEET exam. You had chosen to *live* in Mumbai. You have chosen to *be* the financial support."

"Right," I couldn't say anything else. As much as I wanted to be strong, my own father saying that to me hit like a bullet in my heart. As much as I wanted to shout at him for being the *worst* father ever, I couldn't.

"We gave you another chance, we asked you to help Shanaya with Siddhant. We would have been the happiest, your sister would have been the happiest." *Did they ever care if I was the happiest? Did they ever care what I felt for Siddhant?*

Before I could answer anything, I felt a pair of arms pulling me. He looked at dad in the eye before kissing me on the forehead, and coming closer to my face.

"As much as I hate to confess it here, ***I love you, Kiara. And I'll love you enough for everyone who hasn't, and should have. I'll love you so much that you'll never feel what the word unloved is.*** And I swear if this guy wasn't your father, he would have been shot in the skull." He whispered and I closed my eyes. *This is exactly what I needed. The strength.*

"You'll always have me behind you. You'll always find me passing you the lighter for burning down the world and clearing it for you as well." He winked before he looked at dad.

Siddhant was here. The feeling of ***having somebody behind me****. The feeling of having somebody who'll* ***clear the ashes*** *when I burn the ground down*. The feeling of being belonged, and it wasn't for anything in return.

"I am not at all sorry sir, when I say that I'm in love with the better daughter of yours. Now if you excuse us," I went inside mom's ward and he followed me. I could see Shanaya gritting her teeth looking at us, but it didn't matter to me anymore.

"Kiara,"

"How are you, mom?" I asked and she nodded. "It was a minor attack," I sighed and she pressed my hand. "Siddhant- why is he here?" She looked at me, paranoid seeing him. "He's family." I answered and he smiled. "I'm not sure if I'll ever meet you again, so take care." I kissed mom's forehead and left. Siddhant followed me and glared at dad when he came in front of me.

He clicked on his phone and a notification appeared on Shanaya's phone. "Here's your part done." He nodded at her. "I've appointed an extra nurse to take care of mom until she's fine. Here's my job done as an outsider, now please excuse me." I coerced and went outside. Dad and Shanaya kept looking at me but I didn't stop before the lift gate closed.

"Sid, will you mind if I go out alone for a while?"

"Not at all, love." He passed me the keys to his ford and we reached outside. "Let me know if you need me." I nodded and left.

SIDDHANT

She needed alone time. Everything had turned so overwhelming to her, her family, my confession. She needed some time to think.

I felt light, I felt contended. I had confessed my feelings to her and I was happy. I looked at her drive away and turned back to find two idiots glaring at me. I gulped and smiled.

"How are we going home?" Aryan asked me and I shook my head. "I've texted."

"Whom?"

"The driver, idiot." I rolled my eyes and we waited.

I didn't know what she was going to do.

I didn't know if she was fine with my love.

I didn't know if she loved me back or not.

All I had to do, was wait for her to come *home*.

Chapter 30

SIDDHANT

It had been 3 hours since Kiara had left. Her phone was unreachable now and I didn't feel nice about it. Was there something wrong?

Is Kiara okay?

"She's a big girl." Aryan pacified me and Adhya. She was freaking out just knowing that it had been three hours. I opened my car's location to check where she was, I had to go see her once. Maybe she went to her place and wanted to rest for a while.

"What happened, Sid?" Aryan came and peeped into my phone as my heartbeat raced. I choked on air seeing the location. It was a factory, Oberoi's factory. And for the first time, I felt scared to my core.

I paced from here to there making a plan in my head, Kiara wasn't fine there. And it was surely Rohan Oberoi's plan to take revenge from me. *How could I forget him!* He didn't even have the resources to fund himself, how did he do that? I can't go there directly, because Strawberry wasn't safe. I didn't know what was inside, I didn't know how many people were there.

I didn't know what he wanted.

My phone rang and I already knew who it was. "Remember me, Mr. Goenka?" I heard Rohan's voice, raucous. "Where's Kiara?"

"Oh, so you know she's here." He exclaimed on my question and I punched the table. Aryan pulled my hands back and nodded. *I need to be calm.*

"WHERE IS MY FUCKING GIRLFRIEND?" I growled. "Ah, she's fine. Transfer your company to my name and she'll be all fine."

"***Touch Kiara and I'll make her bathe into your blood.***" I threatened, my voice hoarse. "We'll see to that, Goenka. Look, I've video called you."

I quickly picked up the video call. Rohan Oberoi was a stupid son-of-a-wealthy brat. All he needed was money. He showed me around the place which looked like the first floor and I saw 10 men around him.

Noted.

He finally pointed the camera at Kiara who was tied to the chair as she tried untying herself.

"Being a dick won't make yours any bigger!" Kiara groaned and I smiled. This woman wasn't just strong, but wouldn't flinch to shoot him if she gets a chance. "Strawberry,"

"Siddhant, don't you dare give him the property."

"I have to save you, love." I answered and Rohan pointed the camera back at his place. "Transfer the shares, quick."

Aryan looked at me and I passed him the phone. "I'll do it, it'll take an hour, I need Kiara back."

"Pick her up from the place you destroyed, Goenka!" Rohan's lips twitched into a smirk, *as if he knew he'd won.* I looked at Aryan as the call hung up, "Get the cops ready, I'll go inside alone."

"You're not going alone," Aryan reprimanded and stopped me from moving. "Aryan, I need to make sure Kiara is fine." My voice dripped with fear. I didn't *care* what happened to anyone else in the world, *except for Kiara*. And right now, she was in danger.

"Listen to me, you are not any Christian Harper, I'm calling the security for you." Aryan huffed and I wondered *who the hell was Christian Harper*. He opened his phone and I raised my brow curious to know who he called. He smiled and I heard the phone being picked up.

"Good evening, Mr. Sharma," I heard a silvery voice say. "Good evening Mrs. Singhania, are you still in the business?"

"Of course I am, tell me what you need." *Wait, it was Samaira Mittal Singhania*, well I cannot be more proud of Aryan's choices right now. "Samaira, hey,"

"Siddhant, long time, anyway, what is it?" Aryan explained the situation to her and she hummed. "My team will be there, nobody will know. Siddhant, make sure to not go there without security outside," She instructed and I nodded. My throat dried as the time passed.

I entered the building, my movement steady. I had to save Kiara, no matter whatever it took. I reached the gate as two humans came near me to tie my hands. They took me inside, and the first thing I saw was Rohan Oberoi laughing with Kiara Ahuja.

Wait. What?

He looked at me and his eyes brightened. Kiara passed me another look of surprise. “Didn’t expect us to fool you, Goenka?”

“IQ of 150, bullshit.” Kiara chimed in. I looked at her, my gaze questioning and demanding. Rohan asked his people to tie me on the chair and looked at Kiara who smirked. “Let’s just kill him and end the matter here,” She enjoined and cocked the gun, placing it under my chin. Terror for her inside me changed into numbness, and I didn’t have any emotions left to decipher.

Was she betraying me all this time? My question never came out. I didn’t care, it didn’t matter. Rohan glared at me before he kicked my chair and it broke, making me fall down on the floor. “That’s your place, you piece of shit.” He spat and I got up, my hands free now.

Kiara’s eyes were laced with ice as she pointed the gun towards me again. “Let’s give you options, Kiara, my dear,” Rohan’s voice laced with honey.

“Can we have all the options where he is dead?” She bargained and I smiled. “I didn’t speak a word until now, but since Rohan is such a stupid, do you really think I’ll transfer all my shares to you?” I gazed at Kiara whose hands shuddered on the gun. Rohan snickered, "Who cares after you're dead?"

I chuckled, my laugh sarcastic and taunting. It didn't matter for whom it was. As if I cared. Kiara Ahuja did not love me, and it was clear.

"Heart or brain, baby?" Rohan kissed Kiara's shoulder blade from behind. "Choose the heart, Strawberry." I affirmed. I closed my eyes as I didn't want *anyone else* kissing Kiara to be the last thing I saw.

Green eyes. Chocolate hair. Velvet scent.

Time slowed down as her laugh passed through my mind. The way her eyes shined seeing me on the date. The way we kissed. The way we laughed. The way we hated. *Everything about her had been magical to me.*

A loud gunshot is what I heard before I flinched and fell down on my back. The bullet was straight towards my chest, but it didn't hit my heart. I couldn't alert the security before they ran outside from the back door. I silently shifted and found the gun fallen near me when they started running away.

I picked up the gun and pointed towards them, Kiara following Rohan. Even if I had the gun in my hands *I couldn't fire at her.*

Chapter 31

SIDDHANT

I reached for my phone and clicked on the button they had provided me and the team entered. Aryan and Adhya were leading the pack as he quickly sat beside me and helped me sit up. He opened the shirt I wore and helped me take off the jacket they had made me wear.

Samaira Mittal was a genius about the bullet proof jacket. Adhya looked at the bullet right in the middle of the chest and I smiled. "The bullet has impacted his brain I guess." She exclaimed and Aryan raised his brows at me.

"Kiara shot you?" I heard a strong voice from behind as Samaira entered with a tab in her hands. "Kiara shot him?" Aryan and Adhya chorused. "You're kidding." Adhya then checked the tab. Their eyes went wide seeing that. "***Kiara loves me.***"

"She SHOT you." Aryan looked at me bewildered but my expressions never changed. "***She didn't shoot me in the heart, Aryan. She loves me.***"

"*Ishq me bawla ho gaya hai yeh!*" Samaira rolled her eyes at me. "GET YOUR MIND AT PLACE SIDDHANT. YOU JUST GOT SHOT." Aryan shouted and made me stand. I shook my head, "Give me the tab, there's a loophole."

We looked at the recording and found a man standing behind me, he had a rifle in his hands as he pointed it directly at my head. Kiara was forced to shoot me, *she was being blackmailed.* She's not even safe.

I got up, "I have to go find her." I felt a hand on my shoulder, holding me back firmly. I looked behind to find Samaira smirking. "He doesn't know that we know. We have to use it."

"What is your plan?" I asked and she nodded. She dialed some people and asked me to follow her. They drove straight towards the Oberoi mansion.

Kiara wasn't fine.

Kiara wasn't safe.

Kiara wasn't stable.

Oh god, please make sure she is fine. I hope Rohan doesn't hurt her. Every nerve of my body wanted me to shoot him, and I am sure Samaira wouldn't deny me doing it.

Samaira Mittal was the daughter of Sameer Mittal, she owned the IT sector. She was the mafia princess, and married the love of her life Ahaan Singhania last year.

She was one of the strongest persons I had met when I was training myself for the IT section.

We reached the Oberoi mansion where her team entered suddenly, shooting every person on their way and leading me and Samaira inside. Adhya and Aryan were sitting in the car.

KIARA

Rohan was laughing as he sat on the chair in front of me. He had taken everything away from me again. And it wasn't even my fault. Sometimes I hate to be alive.

I had shot Siddhant. I don't even know if he was fine.

I had shot Siddhant. I knew if he was fine he'd hate me.

I had shot Siddhant, and I knew I had lost him.

"Kiara, I cannot believe you shot him in the heart." He yammered, and I hated it. I wish I could shoot him in the heart instead.

Blue eyes. The blue eyes staring into mine waiting to see an emotion there. Waiting to know if I loved him back. His heart pained when Rohan kissed my shoulder, and all I felt was disgust. I wish I could tell Siddhant at that moment.

Silent tears left my eyes as he pressed his face into my neck. "I can leave you alive if you choose to be mine."

"I'd rather die." I whimpered, trying to move myself away. He cambered the gun, pressing it on my jaw. "Then ready to say goodbye?"

Blue eyes. Spicy vinegar scent. Black hair.

Out of all the people I would want to die for, he took the first place. And he would always be the first. Seven minutes before I lose my life, and it would all have him.

A bullet sound hammered my ear and I waited for the pain to fill me but it never happened. A strong embrace pulled me and the *spicy scent* filled me. I shuddered under the touch and my trapped breath left me. My sobs broke and he pulled me closer. "You're safe. You're fine." He assured himself more than he assured me.

Picking me up, he took me outside and made me sit. I finally opened my eyes to look at his face, kissing my forehead softly. "I love you, Siddhant. I love you, I am so sorry-" I hiccuped as he pulled me closer and patted my back, his touch light as a feather. "Strawberry, I know, calm down."

"He- he threatened me..." I explained and he patted my back. "Baby, I know, please,"

"Sid, all clear." I looked behind to find IT queen Samaira Mittal standing with a gun in her hands. A gasp escaped my throat and she smiled. "How are you, Kiara?" She asked, her voice sweeter than honey. *With that gun in hand,* she didn't look like she'd shoot somebody. "I'm okay-"

"Samaira is an old batchmate,"

"And a don?" I asked and they looked at each other before laughing. "Very few people know about that darling, and make sure to not say it out loud." She emphasized on *few* and *loud* and I nodded quickly. So she was a DON? She can't be a don, she had police with her.

"Thank you, Samaira." Siddhant and Samaira side-hugged before she looked at me and smiled. "Take care of yourself, and believe." She pressed my hands tightly and I sighed, nodding.

I looked at Siddhant, who sat beside me after she left. "Are you okay?" It didn't look like he was shot, at all. "I'm fine, I was protected." I sighed hearing him. He wasn't really shot.

"You're really strong, Strawberry. Look, you won all the battles of your life today." He cheered and simpered. I placed my hands on his neck as his head dipped in my direction, "Not the last one, until now." And I pressed my lips on his.

Rough and desperate. His lips felt miserable, the kiss felt urgent. "I love you, Siddhant Goenka!" I whispered and his lips curved into a big smile. He leaned in again to kiss me, our eyes shining before a familiar throat clearing shattered the moment.

I broke the kiss and beheld Adhya and Aryan eyeballing us. "Finally!" Adhya engulfed me in a big bear hug and I cackled. Siddhant got up and Aryan hugged him. He broke the hug within seconds, pushing him away.

"Sid, come on yaar!" Aryan whined. Adhya and I chortled as she pulled everyone in a group hug.

After a long time, *I felt complete*.

Siddhant was ***mine***.

And I was all ***his***.

Chapter 32

SIDDHANT

Kiara was fine. She was safe.

I assured myself again, as Adhya, Aryan and she chatted happily in the car. I was driving us back, while these three played music and danced.

Everything felt happy, everything felt complete.

In the harmony of life, I've found where I truly belonged. Her love was mine, her love was the light. My heart filled with delight when she finally said those words out aloud. Rightly said, *love conquers every plight*.

Right now, in this moment, in this love divine, I was just grateful that she was mine.

"No way you don't know this song!" I was pulled away from my thoughts by Aryan screaming. "I might have heard it," Kiara answered him. "It is the best song!"

The song hasn't even started properly, it is just the first music. I rolled my eyes as we reached and I stopped the car. “Hey hey hey! The song!” Aryan shouted and I looked at him. “*Kaam karr na apna!*” I nagged him and went outside to open the door for the girls. Adhya and Kiara laughed seeing Aryan sulk and we went inside.

“Sid, I need to discuss something.” I nodded at Aryan. Adhya and Kiara had gone to freshen up and we boys sat outside. “I am planning to propose Adhya,”

“Fuck what-” I looked at him bewildered again. He smiled and nodded. I grinned, the delight doubling inside my heart. “Oh good God, you grew up.” He rolled his eyes and pulled me in a hug. I didn’t deny that. “We’re going home for Diwali, so I’m inviting Adhya to meet my parents, I’ll propose there.” He elaborated and I nodded.

“I cannot wait, now.” I patted his back and the girls came outside. “Cannot wait for what?” Adhya asked and I shook my head. “We’re going home for Diwali, and we want you guys to come.” I requested.

“Diwali-” Kiara mumbled and I pulled her on my lap. She glared at me before I shrugged. “Sharma uncle and aunty are cooler than Aryan, I promise.” Adhya snickered and Aryan frowned, his eyes narrowed.

“I am quite nervous,” Adhya smiled and Aryan rested his head on her lap, lying on the couch. “Don’t worry, they will love you.”

“I am hungry,” Kiara pouted and I smiled. “Let’s go cook,” I picked her up and strolled to the kitchen. Her mouth turned into a grin when I made her sit on the platform and started finding stuff. “Sharma’s, they’re like your parents too, right?”

"Yes," I told her honestly, there was nothing I ever wanted to not be able to speak to her. "They have been taking care of me since school, and are more than parents to me." She grabbed my arm and pulled me towards her. Kissing my forehead, she pecked my lips, "I would love to meet them."

We finished cooking with a lot more giggles and laughter. Aryan and Adhya joined us and everything felt complete. I felt contended, *something that I felt after quite a while*.

"When are we leaving then?" Kiara asked and Aryan opened his phone. "I'll book the tickets, the day after tomorrow?" I asked and Adhya nodded. "I'll finish work,"

"How is the movie going on?" I looked at Aryan who looked at Adhya. "He is rarely focused on the movie,"

"Because I just focus on you," Aryan smirked and Kiara looked at me. Her eyes shined seeing her best friend all giddy, and I controlled a laugh seeing him flirt. Aryan was *whipped* for Adhya.

"Uhm, uh-" Adhya blushed, "The movie is going perfect. We're all set for the release on Valentine's day." She answered my question. I smiled teasingly at Kiara who raised her hands to circle around both of them before twisting them at her head.

Aunty would love her. I smiled seeing her do the tradition and wiped off the food on her lips.

"I'll drop Adhya and go to my place, see you later." Kiara kissed my cheek and waved at Aryan before she went outside. I had already got her car ready since I had to go to Goenka Group. I looked at Aryan once before leaving, and he seemed to move towards the library to work by himself.

Chapter 33

KIARA

We were at the Indore Airport, the place where Aryan's parents lived. It was as exciting as making-me-nervous it was. I had read a book the whole flight ignoring Siddhant, who had slept realizing I wouldn't budge.

I had clicked a hundred pictures of him sleeping cutely, leaving my book for a while. We reached outside and a cab waited for us. I wasn't sure if they were going to like me, but I hope they do. They mattered to Siddhant a lot, and thus it mattered to me.

The house was gorgeous as we got down from the cab and looked at it. Aryan and Siddhant sighed looking at it and then passed their hands to us. Adhya held Aryan's hand softly while I intertwined mine with Siddhant's. We reached the gate and saw Aryan's parents' faces lit up seeing them. They came running towards the gate and saw us.

"Oh my god!" Aunty covered her mouth in surprise as she saw our hands. Uncle just smiled at us. "Siddhant!" She hugged him first as I left his hand letting him pull her closer. He touched her feet after breaking the hug and then she hugged Aryan. Siddhant touched uncle's feet and looked at me.

I was about to bend down to touch their feet when Aunty stopped me. "Bacche, daughters don't touch feet." She caressed my face softly and hugged me.

It didn't matter if she wasn't Siddhant's mother, she loved him more than her own son. And she was already the most loving woman I had met. In the corner of my heart, I wished my mom was as loving as her, or maybe I was their younger child.

Uncle patted my head softly and then they met Adhya. "Best diwali presents, by the way." Aunty exclaimed looking at us. Aryan and Siddhant passed a lopsided grin to us before looking back at her. "Maa, papa, she is Adhya Verma," Aryan introduced and Adhya smiled at them nervously.

"And this is Kiara Ahuja," Siddhant looked at me and I grinned shyly. "You are the most dedicated lover I have seen after Ram," Aunty slapped Siddhant's head and I looked at him wide-eyed. "Kiara, we have known you since your internship days," Ram Uncle looked at me, clearing my confusion.

I shook my head as he nodded softly. I felt giddy, but more affirmed than it could ever. He had told his parents everything, since the internship days. I was still confused, did he tell them I rejected him too? Shouldn't they not-like me?

"Kiara, Adhya, come I'll show you your rooms." Aunty grinned at us and we nodded. Siddhant and Aryan looked at Uncle who smirked. "Sakshi, tell your sons they don't get to share a room with their girlfriends."

"Yeah we're not that modern!" Aunty teased the boys and we chuckled. "Aunty, I'll take the bag," I tried taking the suitcase when she went towards it. "Don't worry bacche, even I ain't picking it up. Siddhu, Aru, take the bags."

I smirked at Siddhant, and he smiled. He felt content, seeing me and aunty laugh. Aunty took us to the two rooms on the floor above, with the boys following. "Thank you maa," Aryan kissed aunty's cheek and grinned.

"You're here for Diwali, and I don't want to be a grandmother this soon, okay?" She commanded and I smirked at Adhya. "Siddhu, especially take care." She looked at Siddhant and his eyes widened. Aunty chuckled looking at my face and we kept out stuff inside.

"Freshen up and I'll see you at lunch," She caressed Adhya's back before leaving. I went inside Siddhant's room and smiled. "Mom loves you," He kissed my forehead. "I don't know how to cook really well,"

"Don't worry," He chuckled, hearing my doubt. "I'm the one who cooks," He winked and I smiled. "Let's freshen up."

I didn't wear a lot of traditional clothing, but kurti was one of my comfort clothes to wear. I wore a pink floral print A-line kurti with white palazzo pants. Siddhant came outside and looked at me. "My fucking-" He didn't even complete his words and back hugged me. I looked at him, "Get away I have to get ready."

"Fuck the lunch," He whispered, his voice husky. Siddhant kissed my earlobe before turning me towards himself, "I'm already-"

"Shush," I placed my finger on his lips and pushed him back. "Wear your clothes and come downstairs." I kissed his neck and ran outside. He shook his head and picked up his shirt.

We all had lunch. Aunty and Uncle told us about Siddhant and Aryan's childhood and how they were inseparable. They said they were glad to see us and appreciated our patience with their boys. Adhya and I were the happiest to meet them, they were loving and amazing.

Everyone was done with dinner and I was about to go out when Siddhant pulled me back. "What?"

"You can't go outside,"

"Why?"

"Because Aryan is proposing to Adhya!" He affirmed and my eyes lit up. *What!?*

Aryan was proposing to Adhya, my best friend was going to get married. OH MY GOD! My freaking freak ass couldn't wait for a moment and I slipped outside to hide and see them. Siddhant pressed his forehead before following me.

I wasn't that late, I guess...

"Adhya Verma, will you marry me?" Aryan took out the ring and Adhya's eyes shimmered with tears. She looked at him, and nodded softly. "Yes."

"Yes! Oh my god yes!" I was about to shout when a hand covered my mouth and looked at me. "Strawberry," He smiled helplessly while I started crying seeing them.

"My best friend is going to get married." I recited and he nodded. "Same, babygirl!" He chuckled. We slipped back inside, leaving the two love birds to kiss. Aunty and Uncle saw us and raised their brows.

"He did it!" Siddhant exclaimed and Aunty and Uncle jumped in delight.

Who said I didn't have a family!

Siddhant and his world was the family I craved.

He had been the comfort, the solace, the love I ever wanted, as much as I hated that it was him.

He was the reason for my *anger*, and I hated that he was the ***only reason to be calm.***

He was the reason for my *sleepless nights*, and I hated that his ***love was the reason I couldn't sleep.***

He was my *biggest competition*, and I hated that ***he won all of it.***

Siddhant saved me from my own self.

He made me realize how the feeling of contentment felt.

He made me realize how the feeling of belonging felt.

He made me realize how the feeling of being in love felt.

Once I hated to be jealous of his *delusional heart*, and now I ***love*** his *heart*.

Siddhant wasn't a cigarette, he was the only ***addiction*** *I needed.*

EPILOGUE

SIDDHANT

Aryan and Adhya were getting married today. Adhya had always wanted to do a Christian wedding, and my best friend wanted to fulfill every wish she had. Everyone was walking here and there to make sure everything was perfect.

Kiara had taken the job to be their wedding planner and no imperfections were allowed when my Strawberry was doing a job. She screamed and ordered everyone to check everything was ready. In a beautiful baby pink dress, she looked euphoric. More than everyone else, I was nervous.

Why? Because I was proposing to Kiara after the wedding today. I was sure since the day I saw her, *she was mine to be*. It didn't matter how much time we took, we were together and that's all mattered. Everyone was ready and I went to Aryan.

Adhya already knew about my plan and she was more than excited to see me propose than her own wedding. *That's how best friends are.* Right! Now I accept it.

"All set?" I asked adjusting Aryan's bow tie and he nodded. "Nervous, but okay."

Adhya's parents had been quite comfortable with Aryan, *his charms worked.* Everyone settled down and I walked towards Kiara, as she held my bicep while I walked her towards the stage. I stood beside Aryan, *I was the only best man he needed.*

Aryan was getting married. My best friend was getting married and I couldn't be more happier as it was the love of his life. His eyes glistened as he saw Adhya walking down the aisle with her father. I patted his shoulder softly, as he smiled looking at her.

Her face radiated delight, her eyes shining. They both looked into each other's eyes and my eyes connected to Kiara's. Her eyes shimmered with tears seeing her best friend marrying.

"Dearly Beloved, we are gathered here today to celebrate Aryan Sharma and Adhya Verma in holy matrimony..." The speech continued, and my eyes never left staring at the green beautiful orbs. It didn't matter what happened in the future, I was always going to be there beside Kiara.

We all cheered as Adhya and Aryan kissed softly. They met their parents and then hugged us.

"Good God! Congratulations you two!" Kiara squealed excitedly. I hugged Aryan and patted his back, "Stay joyous, you both!" I wished and they grinned at me.

She was talking to Samaira when I hugged her from behind, her velvet scent filling me. "You look mesmerizing, Strawberry."

"Mm hmm," She hummed and looked at me. Her face glowed in delight. "Am I being missed?" I looked at Ahaan Singhania, joining Samaira. Ahaan Singhania was one of the biggest actors in the industry and Samaira and him had been childhood sweethearts. They had a rollercoaster ride with their life and had been happily married.

"Oh my god, she's so cute!" Kiara exclaimed, seeing the angel in Ahaan's arms. "Aira," Samaira cooed and Kiara took the baby girl in her arms. "Aww, such a beautiful name," She exclaimed and played with the baby. "Goenka!"

"Singhania!" We nodded at each other and Kiara smiled. "Nod your heads one day, please."

"I know right," Aryan chimed in and they laughed. "I am sure it's not too late to join in?" I heard a deep voice say.

Kiaan Roy, the technical brain of Alpha IT, one of the biggest IT companies of India. I had met him often at the events I attended, and Aryan and him were quite good friends. Aryan had known him through Kiaan's wife, who was a colleague in Aryan's internship.

"Kiaan, hey!" Aryan and he hugged. He then met Adhya while everyone was talking. As the time approached, my nervousness increased.

Adhya stood turning back, with a bouquet ready in her hands. She was about to toss it as all the girls stood behind her, while I stood right behind, as it was the time to propose.

Green eyes. Chocolate hair. Baby pink dress.

Adhya suddenly turned and walked towards Kiara, giving the bouquet to her softly. Kiara looked at her, confused and turned back to find me sitting on my knees.

Her mouth fell open as she covered it with the free hand she had. Her eyes swam with tears as she looked at me, lovingly.

"I knew I was in love the day I saw you in the internship in that red dress. It didn't matter how much time you needed, I was always in love with you. And as I sit here trying to find the right words to express, I am short of them. From the moment our eyes first met, I knew those green eyes would have my heart forever.

Strawberry, you're the light to my darkest days, the warmth I ever needed and the melody that plays in my heart with every beat. You make me happier than I ever thought I could ever be.

I want you to know that you're my everything, the reason for my calm slumber, my reason to smile, my reason to live.

So, my love, I want to make you feel the same way, and love you for the rest of my life, until the end of time.

Ms. Kiara Ahuja, will you marry me?" I looked at her as tears ran down her eyes and she softly bent down dipping her head placing her softer than cotton lips on mine.

"Yes, Siddhant. A million times over!" She answered and my smile turned wider. I made her wear the ring and she jumped into my arms, tossing the bouquet in the air and letting the roses fall all over us.

"***In all the world there is no heart for me like yours to love,***" She said against my mouth. "***In all the world, there is no love for you like mine.***" I finished and kissed her again.

Kiara was mine.

Strawberry, was all mine, forever.

With her, I was complete.

ACKNOWLEDGEMENT

I am immensely grateful to everyone who has been a part of this journey and has contributed to the creation of this book. Their support, encouragement, and guidance have been invaluable.

I would like to express my deepest gratitude to my family, for their unwavering love, understanding and patience throughout this process. Mom and dad, thank you for always loving me and being the best parents.

A big thank you to my friends, who provided continuous support and cheered me on every step of the way.
PS- Moon, Rush, JD, Janhavi, Aru, Divu, EB, you guys <3

For and always, the moon, who shone bright in the sky and always gave me the solace to write and believe in the beauty of scars.

The team at Blue Rose, for their professionalism and dedication in bringing this book to life.

I am grateful for the readers and supporters of my work, whose enthusiasm and feedback have motivated me to keep writing.

Lastly, I want to thank all the authors and books that have inspired and influenced me.

This book would have been impossible without the contributions of each and every one of you. Thank you for being a part of this incredible journey.

ABOUT THE AUTHOR

Kajal Kukreja is a girl who falls in love with characters more than people. She spent most of her days in an ethereal realm, where imagination painted the cityscape with aesthetic wonders.

She finds solace in little things; looking at the world from the perspectives of every kind of human is something she craves. She remembers everything in detail, so you'll always find her drowned in thoughts.

An absolute admirer of books, she can be found dancing if not working. If you're in any dilemma being a writer or reader, you can reach out to her on Instagram. (@kajal._.writes)

ABOUT THE AUTHOR

[illegible]

www.ingramcontent.com/pod-product-compliance
Lightning Source LLC
LaVergne TN
LVHW041935070526
838199LV00051BA/2796
9789364529563